THE SECOND STORY THEATRE

THE SECOND STORY THEATRE

AND TWO ENCORES

BY JAMES BROWN

STORY LINE PRESS

1994

© 1994 by James Brown
First American Printing

All rights reserved. No part of this book may be reproduced in any form or by any electronic or mechanical means including information storage and retrieval systems without permission in writing from the publisher, except by a reviewer.

ISBN: 0-934257-49-3
Published by Story Line Press, Inc., Three Oaks Farm, Brownsville, OR 97327

This publication was made possible thanks in part to the generous support of the Nicholas Roerich Museum, the Andrew W. Mellon Foundation, and our individual contributors.

For their kindness, their friendship and guidance, I thank Lisa Bankoff, Donald Heiney, Harry Hellenbrand, Stephanie Mann, Robert and Lysa McDowell, Tim O'Brien, Art Monterastelli, Peter Schroeder and, as always, Orlando Ramirez.

Portions of *The Second Story Theatre* have appeared in slightly different form in the *Southern California Anthology* and *Point West*. "The Rat Boy" received a Nelson Algren Award in Short Fiction and was published in the *Chicago Tribune Book Review*. "The Friend" will be published in *Other Voices* (University of Illinois at Chicago) in 1994.

For Heidi and our sons Andrew and Logan

TABLE OF CONTENTS

THE SECOND STORY THEATRE 9

THE RAT BOY 133

THE FRIEND 161

THE SECOND STORY THEATRE

1

They were getting closer. Each time the iron ball hit, he felt the tremor move through the streets, come up through the floorboards and pass through his bones. He went to straighten the framed poster from *Pearl of Blood*, but it was no use. Each time the iron ball hit, it only went askew again. Henry reached for his glass of burgundy on the TV tray and took a sip. The bottle in the kitchen was nearly empty, he'd have to buy another soon, but the market where he had once shopped was no longer standing. Now he had to pull his cart a good mile to the next nearest grocery store—a goddamned supermarket, another Ralph's. He resented the big markets with the packaged meats, the long lines, the irate checkers and the impatient stares of the customers as he searched through his coin purse for the right change. Faintly, in the distance, he heard the sharp burst of a whistle, and a moment later the tractors and bulldozers clattered to a halt. He picked up the letter on the TV tray and read it again, for the third time that afternoon.

> State of California
> Department of Transportation
> City of Los Angeles Division

> Dear Mr. Henry Martin:

> Your recent request to remain in the two-story residential dwelling at 421 Norwell has been denied by board officers. Under Section 14, Article I of the California Constitution, Law of Eminent Domain, you are obligated to vacate said dwelling immediately upon notice. A Declaration of Eviction has been filed with the court, and failure to comply will result in a six-month jail sentence, a fine of up to $1000, or both.

> (signed)
> Jacob Waters
> Superintendent of Roads & Highways
> Department of Transportation

He dropped the letter, grabbed up his pen and began to write on a pad of paper.

> Mr. Jacob Waters:

> I've lived in my house 28 years and now you tell me I have to move. Mr. Waters, you can take your freeway and shove it up your ass because this is one man who isn't about to kowtow to your shit or anyone else's.

> Sincerely,
> (signed)
> Henry Martin
> Home Owner

He signed his name with a flare, pressing the pen deep into the paper, running the ink high on the last letter. Just as he finished, he looked up and saw two men in hardhats pass on the sidewalk in front of his porch. One carried a lunchbox and the other was laughing and smoking a cigarette. Henry watched them until they'd disappeared up the block, then he found an envelope, slipped the letter inside and poured himself another glass of wine. That night, as he lay in bed unable to sleep, he heard his roommate, Eddie, pacing the floor above him. Seconds later came the clatter of a typewriter. Long silences followed, then more clatter, then more pacing.

Henry rolled over and switched on the bed lamp. Two masks that he'd worn in *Swamp Monster*, grotesque faces covered with shiny scales, stared down at him from where they hung on the wall over his dresser. He stared back. The eyes were empty, black pinholes. Hot bile rose from his belly to his chest and he winced, reached for the bottle of Maalox on the nightstand, uncapped it and drank. It was the wine coming back on him, all the cheap wine turned sour. Someday, he thought, the stuff might even kill him; if not that, the goddamned Maalox surely would. He looked down at his arm in the dim light of the bed lamp and took notice of his copper bracelet and how it had turned his wrist a pale, dusty green. Between the two fingers where he held his cigarettes, the skin was stained a dark orange, and the muscles of his forearm, once powerful and taut, had long since drawn into themselves. Still, he thought, he was plenty strong. His mouth felt dry, his throat raw. Henry climbed out of bed and slipped on his bathrobe. As he went to get himself a glass of water, he passed the living room window when something bright, something shining caught his eye and he stopped. For a moment he could've sworn that he'd seen a light flash in the window of the Gold Room several blocks away. Henry blinked. He shook his head and looked harder. But the light, or whatever it may have been, was gone. His eyes were weak and not to be trusted.

The Royal Hotel had been boarded up now for over a year.

2

Just as Bela Lugosi was known throughout the world as Dracula, as Buster Crabbe was Buck Rogers, Eddie Shapiro had become Linus. Every Christmas and Halloween millions of children across the country listened to his nasal voice while they watched the Peanuts character perform with thumb-in-mouth. The money was good, it'd come at a time when he needed it badly, but now he often wished that he'd done without. Kids who overheard him talking recognized his voice and at first the attention flattered him and he accepted the role proudly. Occasionally he signed an autograph on the back of a napkin, or on a scrap of paper found on the floor, and sometimes he even stuck his thumb in his mouth, threw his sweater over his shoulder as if it were Linus' security blanket and did an impersonation for the kids.

That was all right, that was fun. He enjoyed making them laugh and smile. It was all the casting agents, the producers, all the ones who would no longer hire him that Eddie had grown to resent and eventually fear. As a child he'd worked regularly, but by twenty-six he hadn't been able to land more than a walk-on.

He lived upstairs, in the part of the house Henry converted into a theatre, and this morning while he lay belly down on the sofa bed he thought about his play. It was the first that he'd written, and he figured it would be the last before the Second Story Theatre was shut down. At the foot of the bed rested a copy of the *Player's Directory*, which he'd been studying the night before, and now he reached for it again. A sheet of paper was clipped to the cover.

THE ROYAL HOTEL

Gary Lombardo . . . . hotel owner
Lily Hill . . . . mistress
Bert Goodman . . . . elevator operator

He flipped it open to the Leading Women and thumbed through the pages, looking at the different faces until he found two small black-and-white headshots of Evelyn Richardson. In one she wore a bright smile, a pageboy haircut and a turtleneck sweater, and in the other she was frowning, her gray hair pinned up neatly in a bun.

The week before he'd watched her and Henry in a horror movie, an old one that still ran on late night TV every now and then. She'd played the harried counselor to a group of Girl Scouts on a weekend trip, when they discover a colony of dwarf-like creatures living in the Malibu hills. *Beyond the Forest* was the name of the film, and Henry's role in it had been that of the camp maintenance man. There was a framed still of him and Evelyn on top of the TV in the living room downstairs. Her career had long since blossomed with good roles in better films, lots of Broadway work and too many TV spots. Now she played the lead on a hit series called *Testimony*. Linus rolled out of bed, wandered across the cold dressing room floor and parted the curtains. Rows of metal fold-out chairs filled the little theatre, and above them floodlamps of different sizes and colors ran the length of the stage. The walls were painted flat black. He went to the window at the back of the room and lifted it open and leaned out. In the distance the iron wrecking ball dangled from the cable of a crane in front of the old Royal Hotel and beyond it he could see the concrete ramp hanging in the haze of smog off Highway 101. Soon it would slope to the earth and continue onward, directly through the house he and the old man lived in, where it would link 101 with Interstate 10 on the other side of town.

On the lawn below Henry stood staring up at him. He held a garden hose in one hand. He was watering his roses. "Finally decided to get your ass out of bed?" he said. Linus leaned over the windowsill and shouted back.

"We need to talk."

"About what?"

"I'll be right down."

A minute later he was dressed, all except for his tennis shoes, and had hurried downstairs. He straddled the porch railing. "Were you and Richardson friends?"

"Who?"

"Evelyn Richardson," he said. "Think she'd remember you?"

The old man looked up from the roses and stared at him. No answer was necessary. Then he turned away and lifted a leaf on one of the rose bushes. It had some kind of white rot, some kind of fungus growing on the underside. He yanked it off.

"What're you talking about? I'm the guy who showed her how to snarl," he said, "the one everyone knows her for." He nodded. "Me. I taught her."

"She'd make a great Lily Hill."

"You're out of your mind."

"She's your friend."

"You don't ask friends those kinds of favors."

"Come on," he said, "we could fill the theatre with her."

They'd never had much of an audience. Twenty-two was the most Linus could remember them ever drawing and half of those had been people he'd dragged off the streets minutes before the curtain.

"This might be the last time we work together," he said. "Why go to all the trouble of putting on another play if nobody's going to come? Just give her a copy of the script and I'll shut up." He paused. "You got her number?"

Henry shook his head.

"Her address?"

Again he shook his head.

"You know anyone who even knows her?"

He raised the hose. Linus beat it up the stairs for cover.

"Pick me a dozen roses," Henry hollered, "then get yourself into some decent clothes."

3

Exhaust poured out of the tail pipe as they drove down the street in Linus's beat-up Olds 88. The speedometer needle rose from forty to forty-five. Henry gripped the edge of the seat. "Slow down," he said.

One button of his suit jacket was missing, and the sleeves stopped a couple of inches short of his wrists. And the pants, once left near a window in the sun, no longer matched the color of his coat. It was a shabby suit but it was his best.

"You're going too fast."

"Relax."

"Then slow down."

Linus pressed in the car lighter.

"Have a smoke," he said.

They passed a tattered bed mattress lying on the front porch of an abandoned house. A sheet of splintered plywood, torn from one of the windows, had been tossed into a row of brown, dying shrubs. Chunks of broken glass littered the driveway.

The Olds hit a pothole and the trunk lid banged against the frame. Only rope tied to the rear bumper kept it from flying open. "How come you don't fix that?" Henry said. "I'm sick of hearing it."

"Quit bitching."

"Bitching?" Henry said. "Bitching? It's been broken for months."

He fumbled through his coat pocket for his cigarettes, shook one out and coughed once before he placed it between his lips. When the car lighter popped out, Linus reached for it, but the old man slapped his hand away.

"Just watch the road," he said. "I'm perfectly capable of lighting my own damn cigarettes."

Ornery, Linus thought.

Soon they put the deserted neighborhood behind them and merged with the city traffic into a turning lane.

Henry sat up straight.

"What're you doing?"

"I'm getting on the freeway."

"I don't like freeways."

"It's the fastest way."

"Take the side streets," Henry said. "What's the big hurry?"

But cars had already fallen in behind them, while others sped past on the right. When the light dropped to green, Linus entered the on-ramp and picked up speed.

The front end began to shimmy.

"Christ," he said, "now what's the matter?"

"Nothing."

He stepped on the gas.

"Nothing, my ass. Slow down."

"It smooths out at sixty. I have to go sixty to get rid of the shake."

"You can go a hundred if you want and you can just pull over and let me the hell off, too." He pointed to the side of the highway. "Right here's fine," he said. "I mean it. I'm not ready to die."

"Don't be ridiculous."

Henry clutched the dashboard with one hand. The sleeves of his coat fluttered from the vibrations, as if from a strong wind.

"It wasn't doing it at forty," he said. "Forty's plenty

fast enough."

"Shit, Henry."

"No shit about it," he said. "You just slow her down."

So Linus did as he was told and within seconds the massive grill of a semi appeared in the rearview mirror. He wanted to tell the old man to turn around and look, show him you can't go forty on the Hollywood Freeway without risking your life, but he knew that it would only make matters worse. Instead he sunk down in the seat. Henry stared straight ahead with his lips pursed.

The semi rode their bumper for a solid mile and then, as if to scare them, it sped up suddenly, blasted its horn and switched lanes.

"Stupid son of a bitch," Henry said, as it thundered past them. "Let the fool kill himself. We got enough in the world already."

They drove past a speed limit sign. Linus looked across the seat at him.

"Did you see that?"

"I most certainly did."

"We can get a ticket, you know."

"Fifty-five is the *maximum* speed," he said. "It doesn't mean you have to go that. You're doing just fine at forty." He stubbed his cigarette out in the ashtray. "We're in no rush."

Linus rolled his eyes.

He took the Barham exit and in a couple of minutes they were outside the Burbank Studios. Tall stucco walls surrounded the buildings, and further up the road was Forest Lawn Cemetery. Mausoleums and white gravestones dotted the hillside. It looked like a beautiful place to be buried.

They pulled into the studio's driveway and stopped. A guard stepped out of the booth with a clipboard in his hand.

Henry rolled down the window and smiled.

"We're here to see Evelyn Richardson."

"Your name?"

"Henry Martin."

The guard tipped his hat back and glanced at the clipboard.

"Do you have an appointment?"

"Just give her a call."

"Your name again?"

"Henry," he said, with greater emphasis. "Henry Martin."

The guard returned to the booth. The old man looked at Linus and waved his hand. "Keep the engine running," he said, "this won't take long."

"Did you ever work here?"

Henry frowned.

"What do you think?"

"Calm down," Linus said. "I was just asking."

Ahead they could see the studios, big as warehouses, and the stagehands, Best Boys and extras as they hurried back and forth across the driveway. A flatbed truck hauling dozens of men dressed in battle fatigues turned a corner and disappeared. The guard returned a moment later.

"The A.D. said she's busy."

"We're not here to talk to her A.D."

"I'm sorry."

"Call Tim Horowitz then," the old man said. "Tell him Henry's here."

"Who?"

"He's a big producer here."

"Another friend of yours?"

"That's right."

"Listen, pops. If the A.D. said she's busy, she's busy. And there's no Tim Horowitz on the lot." He slapped the Olds' fender. "Now get this piece of junk outta here."

Henry opened his mouth as if he were about to speak, or curse maybe, but nothing came out, and instead he just rolled up his window. Linus put the car into reverse and they backed out of the driveway. For a while neither of them said a word, but when they were halfway up the block the old man broke the silence.

"Horowitz retired," he said. "It's been a couple years since we talked."

"Hey," Linus said. "It's all right, you tried."

"Don't humor me."

"I'm not humoring you."

"Like hell," he said.

He reached inside his coat and took out his pocket watch. Looked at it. It was almost noon. He pointed to a side street across from the studio.

"Park over there."

"Let's just go back and have a glass of wine."

Henry raised his voice.

"Park it, I said."

Linus sighed, maneuvered the Olds to the curb and shut off the engine. It sputtered and shook, and before it died Henry grabbed up the dozen roses and climbed out of the car. He walked with his chin up, his chest out, with his baggy pants flapping loosely about his ankles.

Linus had to double time it to catch up.

"Forget it," he said, "we'll find someone else. I'm sorry I ever asked."

But the old man had the same look in his eyes that he'd had in the car on the freeway, fixed, determined, with his lips pursed.

"I've worked here," Henry said. "I made these bastards plenty of good money before they locked the doors on me."

At the edge of the driveway he stopped and reached again into his coat for his pocket watch. Now the hands showed precisely twelve noon. Henry peered around the corner. A white limousine with tinted windows idled in front of the guard booth. The license read OKEEFE. Linus tapped him on the shoulder.

"What're you doing?"

"Stay close to me," he said.

First it was only one voice, then came the others, louder, lots of them joking and laughing. When a crowd of stagehands started down the driveway, Henry slipped around the corner.

"Get back here," Linus said.

But the old man had already blended into the crowd, moving upstream, and even if he'd heard him it wouldn't have made any difference, for Henry had no intentions of turning back. Linus swallowed, then stepped into the crowd. Men in blue jeans, some in dirty coveralls, hurried by him and twice he had to do a quick side step to avoid bumping into someone.

"Henry, listen to me," he said, when he'd caught up with him. "I changed my mind." But Henry only lowered his head and kept walking. A group of stagehands parted to make way for them and Linus smiled apologetically as they passed. A second later the white limousine lurched forward, and he spotted the guard on the other side of the driveway, hands on his hips, scanning the crowd.

"We're going to get arrested, you know."

"Quiet."

"I'm going back."

Henry grabbed him by the sleeve and gave him a dirty look. The crowd had begun to thin and now they were walking without cover. Linus glanced over his shoulder.

Henry jerked on the sleeve.

"Don't look around. Act like you belong here, damn it."

Several women in Victorian gowns and carrying parasols passed, and they slipped by them, around the corner of the first studio. Best Boys, grips and extras stood beside a five-gallon coffee pot near the equipment doors.

Henry caught eyes with one and smiled.

"Where are they shooting *Testimony* today?" he said.

"Studio Twelve," the man said.

"Thanks."

They walked on.

"Now that wasn't so hard, was it?" Henry said.

Linus didn't say anything.

The big numbers on the face of the different buildings rose from six to seven to eight, then stopped, and Henry and Linus found themselves staring at an empty dirt lot.

"Must be the other way," Henry said. "C'mon."

They walked back, past the men drinking coffee, until they came to another dirt lot, this one full of dead, potted oaks.

"You sure you know where you're going?" Linus said.

Henry had begun to breathe a little heavily now, and his knees had begun to ache too. But he ignored the kid, he sucked in his stomach and continued on, and soon they were trodding through a deserted town in World War II Europe. The streets were made unevenly with cobblestone, and the signs in the windows of the stores were written in German. A Nazi cross, painted on a brick wall, was riddled with bullet holes. The day was hot, Linus wiped sweat from his brow with the back of his hand, and spoke again.

"You sure you know where we're going?"

Henry cleared his throat. It was parched, and his hair, which he'd taken great care in combing this morning, hung in limp strands. "It's changed some since I was here," he said. "But I know what I'm doing. Just settle down." Henry switched the roses from one arm to his other and walked on. A few minutes later they wandered onto an old west set with a saloon, with louvered, swinging doors and wooden planks in the front. Two big fans used to stir up dust storms stood beside a water trough.

The old man stopped. He groaned.

"You okay?"

"I'm fine."

"Your knees bothering you again?"

"I said I'm fine," Henry said. "Hold these a second."

He handed him the roses, which had already begun to sag and wilt in the hot sun, then sat down, slowly, on the wooden planks. He rubbed his knee.

"You sure you're all right?"

"I'm sitting down to think."

"Can you walk okay?"

Henry wagged his head.

"So I'm old," he said. "I'm not crippled."

"You're not that old."

"Just let me think."

"I think we ought to get out of here."

The old man frowned, got to his feet and continued down the lot, limping a little, favoring his right leg.

Again Linus followed him, from the western set and onto the main driveway again. For some, lunch was nearing its end, and actors, stagehands and others hurried back to work, when Linus and Henry spotted Studio Twelve. A couple of trailers were parked near the door. A bright red light burned overhead.

"This is it," he said. "Straighten up and tuck in your shirt."

Suddenly a buzzer sounded. The red light went off, the door flew open and a short, handsome man rushed out.

There were tears in his eyes and he walked quickly and heatedly. He was rubbing the side of his face with one hand.

A man wearing a baseball cap hurried after him.

"Please, Danny," he said.

"I'm sick of that old bitch."

"Be reasonable."

"You saw it."

"But you're supposed to be dead drunk," the man in the cap said. He'd caught up with him by now. "She had to revive you, Danny," he said, with his arms spread and his palms up. "It's just acting."

Danny stopped and took his hand away from his cheek. The skin was bright red.

"Is this real enough?" he said. "Is it?"

Then he stormed past Henry and Linus, stepped into the trailer and slammed the door behind him. A moment later a small gray-haired woman made her way across the driveway, a young man in tow. He had on a satin tour jacket with *Testimony* embroidered on the back, and he followed her into the other trailer.

"That's her," Henry said.

He bent over and pulled his socks up, for they had worked themselves down from the walking, then he stood straight and tucked in his shirt. He winked at Linus.

He smiled and adjusted his tie.

"Give me the roses," he said.

Henry walked to the trailer and knocked on the door.

The young man answered.

"Yes?"

"I'm here to see Evelyn."

"No visitors."

The door swung shut. Henry looked at Linus, shrugged and knocked again.

A loud voice came from inside.

"Go away."

He knocked harder.

The door opened.

"I'm a friend of hers," he said.

"I don't care who you are."

"Tell her Henry's here."

The young man narrowed his eyes.

"You're the guy who called earlier?"

He leaned outside of the trailer and waved down a passing stagehand.

"Phone security," he hollered. "I don't know how this old bum got on the lot, but I want him off and I want him off now."

Once again the door slammed shut, only this time it was followed by the click of a bolt. Linus slipped an arm around Henry. "C'mon," he said, "let's get out of here." From inside the trailer, as they were walking away, they heard her voice:

"Who was that?"

But by then a plain white car had pulled up alongside them. The security cop reached over the seat and unlocked the back door. "Hop in, boys," he said. "It's a long walk to the front gate."

Henry looked at the man, and if only briefly considered ignoring him and walking on. Instead he raised the roses to his face and inhaled.

Wilted or not, they still smelled sweet.

4

"The new Royal Hotel," read the society pages of the *Los Angeles Times*, "brainchild of financier Gary Lombardo, offers the finest accommodations and entertainment on the West Coast...." Below the article was a picture of Lombardo and Lily Hill, the cigar girl, standing beside a red ribbon tied across the main doors. She was leaning over, smiling, poised to cut the ribbon with a big pair of scissors. Lombardo, dressed impeccably in a three-piece suit, looked on. A young Henry Martin could be seen standing in the background beside a man in a bellhop's cap. It was Bert, the elevator operator, the one who had slipped him an invitation to the opening ceremonies. The year was 1930, and they were both grinning into the camera.

That same year Lombardo was arrested on New Year's Eve when he stepped outside the hotel to watch the fireworks display that he'd arranged for his guests. Lily happened to be reaching into her purse for her compact at that moment, FBI agents thought she was going for a gun, and one of them shot her in the stomach. The bullet passed through her flesh into the leg of a bystander. Then the fireworks went off. Lombardo pounced on the agent as the colored flames burst in the sky and tumbled back to the earth.

They rolled down the marble steps onto the sidewalk, where he wrested the gun from the agent and struck him with it again and again. Another rocket burst overhead. Back-up agents rushed onto the scene and subdued Lombardo but not before they'd beaten him unconscious. He was later convicted on multiple counts of racketeering, extortion, bootlegging, tax evasion, the gangland slaying of Tony Gianti in San Francisco's Chinatown, and was sentenced to thirty-five years at Alcatraz. His property and assets, including the Royal Hotel, were seized by the Internal Revenue Service.

The following morning the *Los Angeles Times* headlined the event:

RINGLEADER LOMBARDO ARRESTED

The hotel was shut down and would've been auctioned off to the highest bidder if Lombardo hadn't had the foresight to transfer title into Lily's name some months before his arrest. When she recovered from her stomach wound, which had put her in the hospital for several long months, with the help of Bert Goodman she re-opened the hotel to much fanfare. The original guests remained faithful for many years, new ones came and went, but eventually the glamour and excitement that the Royal once generated, along with its spirit, began to fade. Major studios had since moved from the city's center to the suburbs of Hollywood, leaving behind the grand cathedral-like theatres—the Los Angeles, the State, the United Artists and the Orpheum—that had once catered to vaudeville and silent film.

Upkeep on the Royal, despite Lily and Bert's efforts, declined until the hotel had finally taken on the appearance of the decaying buildings that now surrounded it. As taxes continued to rise, Lily and Bert turned the Royal into a resident hotel, comprised mostly of pensioners, people down on their luck, and hookers and pimps. Sometimes, with the same goodwill that prompted Lombardo to sponsor food lines in the Great Depression, they allowed a few transients room and board in exchange for a helping hand.

During his incarceration, until his release in 1964, Lombardo and Lily wrote each other regularly. His letters seldom failed to ask about the hotel, how it was succeeding or failing and who, presently, were its guests. But Lily never had the courage to tell him the truth, and instead made up elaborate lies. The governor slept in suite 402 the week before, yet another star had come in for dinner last night, "and God was he obnoxious," they had a big dance planned for Christmas, and always she ended her letters with the wish that he was there for the celebration.

Then Lombardo returned unannounced one day in February. As he walked from the train station to the Royal, and saw what the neighborhood had become, he knew right away he'd been duped. At first he felt anger, then rage, but when he spotted Lily sweeping the marble steps outside the hotel he understood the reason for the lies and he soon forgave her. After all, she was only trying to protect him. She was only trying to keep the dream alive.

A party followed; all the tenants were invited. At

the height of it Lombardo grabbed a bottle of champagne and he and Lily slipped off to the Gold Room and made love on the table, on the bar, then on the floor. It was the first time since the night of his arrest, and it was also his last, for his health collapsed soon afterwards.

Doctors diagnosed the illness as a degenerative bone disease brought on by years of poor food and not enough of it. There was no known cure. For six months he lingered near death in one of the rooms overlooking the city.

Bert fed him whiskey and morphine; Lily spent hours into the night sitting beside him, patting sweat from his forehead with a damp wash cloth, praying, and talking to him even when she knew he could no longer understand her.

In his last days he had vivid hallucinations of the past. One moment he was in his cell, the next he was with Lily, young and handsome again, dancing and laughing. Then he was being watched, or chased, and the rage would rise up inside of him. Sometimes Lily climbed into his bed and wrapped her arms around him until the frightful hallucinations had passed. Other times she simply sat in the chair and cried. Finally one morning Bert came in to give him his shot and found him with his head thrown back, the eyes open but empty. He liked to think that the last thing Lombardo saw were the fireworks exploding into the sky outside the hotel.

A few years later Linus and his mother checked into room 422. He had just turned six. His hair was blond and curly, his eyes were big, and he had a cute button nose. The mother was tall, thin, and given to wearing too much jewelry. His father, a true disciplinarian, was a career army officer whose work kept him moving from one state to another; and this, along with a dull sex life, undermined what from the "git-go," as Linus's mother had put it, was a pretty shaky marriage. When he received orders to relocate from San Diego, California to Las Cruces, New Mexico, his wife refused to go along with him. The divorce followed.

She took her boy to Los Angeles where, in order to conserve their limited funds, they checked into the Royal Hotel. The room was small but clean with a view of the city, and at night Linus liked to stare out the window at the lights in the distance. He missed his father, he missed the life they had once shared, but his mother had plans for him. Big plans. She took him to movies, she took him to plays. She taught him to smile at the snap of her fingers, to frown at the drop of her hand, even to speak deep from his chest so that his voice carried well.

They had pictures taken, sharp eight-by-ten glossies. He attended tap dance classes on Monday and Tuesday, singing on Wednesday, acting lessons on Thursday and fencing taught by a former Olympian on Friday. They found a good agent.

What little spare time Linus had was spent riding the elevator.

"Hurry."

"Where's it today, Eddie?"

He thrust six fingers into the air.

"To the Top?"

"The Top."

"Are you positive?"

"Please. Hurry."

"Yes, sir."

Bert pulled the steel door shut with a solid clang and depressed the lever. The elevator rose with a hum, then jerked to a halt. He opened the door. At the end of the red carpeted hall were two tall doors inlaid with frosted glass that had cherubs and grapevines etched on them.

"The Gold Room, sir," he said, bowing, holding out his hand. "But you're late. It's closed, been closed now for twenty years, sir."

Linus stared at the tall double doors.

"Ghosts," Bert said. "Watch out for the ghosts or they'll get you."

"Uh uh."

Wide eyed. "Oh?"

"You're lying."

Bert crossed his heart with a finger.

"Haven't you seen a ghost before?"

"There's no such thing."

"Now who told you that? You just haven't looked hard enough. They're there. They're everywhere." He patted the boy on the shoulder and smiled. "Only the people who can see the ghosts get to be one. I know it for a fact." He bent down so they were eye to eye. "Ever hear of Gary Lombardo?"

Linus nodded. His mother had once taken him on a cruise around the San Francisco bay, and he remembered the tourist guide talking about this gangster, this Lombardo character, as he pointed through the fog to Alcatraz. Linus shivered.

Bert glanced down the hallway. "Mr. Lombardo used to own this place," he said. "But he got himself in trouble and they locked him up." He held one hand high over his head. "He was a big man. Brave, too, tough as nails and crazy to match. But he was just like you, he didn't believe in ghosts." A long pause. "Not at first, anyway." Bert took the boy's hand in his own and turned the palm up. "When he came back he was old and skinny. His wrist was small around as yours. He was sick." He leaned closer until their faces weren't but a couple of inches apart.

"That's what it took, though. All that time locked up." Bert drew his finger slowly down Linus's palm and whispered into his ear. "No, sir," he said. "He didn't believe until he saw."

He jerked his hand free.

"You're crazy."

The cords in Linus's throat had grown taut, and when he tried to swallow he found that his mouth was too dry.

Bert smiled and stood up straight.

"Mind me now, sir. I kid you not."

For a moment Linus hesitated and then he strutted down the hall to the tall double doors. They were unlocked, and when he opened them and peered inside, he could see only the outline of a long bar and groups of tables and chairs covered with white sheets. Slowly he moved about the room, his arms outstretched, his heart pounding. The smell of dust and something rotten, something moldy was in the air, and he wrinkled his nose.

As his eyes adjusted to the darkness he could make out the color of the pillars spaced around the room—gold—and the color of the bar—again gold. He looked up.

The ceiling was high and rounded, and on it was a mural of nude men and women reclining beside what looked like a lake thick with silver fish leaping out of the painting toward the tables below. Linus stared and stared.

And years later he would think he'd just stared too long and hard at the silver fish, like someone looking into the sun and then seeing the image pulsate when he looked away. Now he lowered his eyes and in the mirror behind the bar the color silver took the form of a pale face with luminescent eyes staring directly into his own. He lost his breath. He spun around.

"Bert," he screamed. "Bert...."

Out the door he ran, bumping into a table, pulling the sheet off on his way. He scrambled down the hall.

"Bert...."

But the elevator was gone.

He leaned on the button with the flat of his hand and listened to it ring and ring and ring in the empty shaft.

Mrs. Shapiro stood waiting on the fourth floor with her arms crossed over her chest.

"Have you seen Eddie?"

"Can't say I have, ma'am."

"He was here a minute ago."

Bert rubbed his chin, glanced around the elevator, then lifted his foot and looked beneath it.

"He isn't here now."

"This is nothing to joke about."

"Now, now, Mrs. Shapiro."

"His dance lesson's at five."

She rushed off down the hall.

Bert called after her.

"Don't you worry yourself sick," he said. "I'll spook the old codger out."

And he did, as he would time and again. Linus never missed a lesson.

When he emerged from the Royal Hotel thirteen months later, after landing his first role in a TV serial, the boy was a skilled entertainer and a firm believer in the power of ghosts.

The bell continued to ring, steady and constant.

Bert looked up at the ceiling of the elevator.

"Coming, coming," he muttered, closing the door, depressing the lever.

The second time Linus checked into the Royal Hotel he was twenty-five years old and flat broke. His room, again 422, which he had requested and by good fortune or not was available, wasn't as he remembered. It seemed smaller and dirtier, and the bed mattress was soft and lumpy. A dark ring of oil, where a previous tenant had rested his head, maybe to read, or maybe only to stare at the ceiling, soiled the wall between the bedposts. Linus threw his suitcase on the bed, went to the dresser mirror and looked at himself. His cute button nose had grown blunt over the years, like a boxer's who'd had the cartilage broken once too many times, his jaws had grown wide and his ear lobes were much too long. His hair was thinning fast and by thirty he expected to be bald on top. But what was worst of all, he thought, as he drew a finger along the side of his nose, was that despite the years and the changes his face had somehow managed to keep its most childlike qualities. It was a little boy's face on a man's body, and in that sense grotesque. He turned away from the mirror and stared out the window. The shade was tattered and yellowed and the fine view of the city outside was now obscured by smog. Linus went to the bed, stretched out and closed his eyes.

As for Mrs. Shapiro, she had long ago spent the money her son had before his career bottomed out, then remarried another army officer and moved to Illinois. All Linus knew about his father was that he was stationed somewhere in Germany.

Bert was dead.

He had hung himself from the chandelier in the Gold Room with the ghosts.

Although Lily hired another man, he drank more than he worked and twice she caught him asleep on the job. But she didn't fire him. Age and loneliness had come to weigh more and more heavily on her until she'd lost all concern for the Royal and its residents. Lombardo was dead. Bert was dead. The good times were over. Each day she struggled to rise from bed, make herself a small breakfast, wash herself, then ride the elevator down to the lobby. There she worked behind the desk until the evening came.

Occasionally Linus stopped on his way up to his room and visited with her. She talked a great deal about her aches and pains but sooner or later she lapsed into more interesting stories about Lombardo and Bert, the grand parties they once threw, and the night it all came to an abrupt end.

"It was on New Year's Eve," she said. "G-men arrested Gary and shot me in the gut." Lily raised her blouse and showed him the scar where the bullet entered. "Then they beat him up. So maybe he did those other things they said but he didn't kill Tony Gianti. Capone's boys did. It was an inside job. Gary was framed. The government," she said, "they just wanted his money like they do everybody else's."

Linus never interrupted the old woman even though

he had heard the story a dozen times. With each telling he just shook his head at the indignity of Lombardo's arrest, gasped at the sight of her scar, and finally he cursed the government.

Then one morning while Linus sat on the couch in the lobby, thumbing through the classifieds, looking for work, a small elderly man in a baggy plaid sports coat wandered past him. He watched the old man go to the bulletin board next to the elevators, reach into his pocket and take out a batch of flyers rolled into a tube. He peeled one off the roll and tacked it onto the board, then turned, waved to Lily, and wandered back outside. Somewhere, someplace, Linus knew he'd seen that face before. Not in the streets, not in the hotel, but in some movie—or maybe it was on TV. But he knew he had seen him. Of that much he was certain.

Linus went to the board and read the flyer:

> The Second Story Theatre is pleased
> to announce casting of Sean Rick's
> one-act play *Visiting Hour*. An actor is
> needed for Richard, 25-30,
> the companion to an elderly gentleman
> confined to a rest home. Auditions will
> be held March 12, 1 P.M. upstairs at 421
> Norwell. Any and all ticket proceeds will
> be divided equally among the actors.

He looked over at Lily and frowned.
"Who was that guy?"
"Henry Martin."
"He an actor?"
"Used to be," she said, "but he got mixed up with the wrong crowd, right here in my hotel, in the Gold Room, him and this big shot Hollywood director. They

had meetings there." She made a sour face. "Henry's a damn commie. Red through and through. I wouldn't have anything to do with him if I were you."

But on March 12 at 12:15 in the afternoon he left his room and headed for the Second Story Theatre. He wore slacks, a white dress shirt and black high top canvas tennis shoes. His hair, short and thinning, was parted carefully down the middle. The discipline and regimentation of a play, he thought, would be good for him. He needed to act again, to be seen, to work with others. Most of all he needed the play to fill his days so he couldn't spend them drinking. Too much time had been wasted staring out the window, drunk. Too much time had been lost pacing the floor, drunk. But the day before the audition he hadn't drank but half of the pint that he'd bought earlier that morning, when the liquor store opened.

Not until Linus was a good ways up the next block, when he saw the numbers on the houses, did he realize he'd passed the theatre and that he had to turn around. He had expected it to be downtown, or in the old industrial part east of Little Tokyo where the artists lived in lofts, or in a vacant warehouse. Instead he found a weather-beaten two-story house planted on the corner of Norwell and Apple in a neighborhood of other older, run-down homes. This couldn't be it, he thought. This was no theatre. He felt inside his shirt pocket and pulled out a slip of paper with the address on it and saw, sure enough, that the numbers matched. His first response was to head straight back to his room and finish off the pint, and he almost did, but instead he collected himself and walked up to the porch.

An arrow cut out of cardboard and painted red was

taped beneath the mailbox. Linus followed it around the corner and climbed a rickety staircase leading up the side of the house. Above the doorway on the landing was another sign, this one was made of wood, and the painted letters were chipped.

WELCOME TO THE SECOND STORY THEATRE

Linus stepped inside. Blue floodlights shone across two wooden chairs and a couch on stage. The floor had been freshly varnished, and the smell of it lingered in the air. He looked around for the old man, for other actors, but he was alone. For a while he thought that maybe no one could find the place, or that maybe they had and simply left, like he'd almost done when he discovered that it was only an old house in a rundown neighborhood. He wondered, as he stood there, if he ought to leave and save himself and the old man some embarrassment while he still had the chance.

Dozens of copies of the play, neatly stacked and collated, rested on a table next to the stage. Taking one, sighing, Linus sat down in the back row and began to read. It was set in the Ferndale Sanitarium in Los Angeles, and the story was about seventy-three year old John Steeple and his son Richard. The old man wanted out of the rest home. But his boy, this ghost of a son who came only to visit, thought otherwise.

They were two good roles and the dialogue was tight and strong. Still Linus probably would've passed if the old man hadn't come out from the dressing room just then. Already he was back on his feet. Already he had his eye on the door.

But seeing Henry there, smiling at him, what could he say?

Linus cleared his throat.

"Where's your bathroom?" he said.

Henry chose him for the role of Richard over the three other actors who showed up that afternoon. Linus moved about the stage with confidence, his voice carried well, and he listened to John Steeple's lines rather than waiting for them to end before delivering his own. In no way, Henry thought, was this kid an amateur. But the kid's eyes were bloodshot and his face bloated from too much liquor.

After he told him the part was his, he added:

"I don't want any drinking before rehearsals. I don't want any drinking before performances. Afterward, fine. Do what you want. But don't go getting so drunk you're too goddamned hung over the next night to do your job. I'm a professional and I expect the same from you. Understood?"

Linus nodded, ashamed. He hadn't known that his drinking was that obvious to others, as nobody had told him anything about it before. From here on out he vowed to limit himself to wine or beer, no more whisky, vodka or gin. That was the stuff that really made your eyes heavy, that really made it hard sometimes to drag yourself out of bed without another shot or two.

The play, he hoped, would keep him busy.

But there were complications beyond his drinking. It was during the second week of rehearsals that the Department of Transportation took possession of the Royal Hotel. A public hearing was held, and most of the local property owners in attendance considered the state's offer for their dilapidated buildings generous. A few argued for more money, but no one except Henry

Martin condemned the project outright. They didn't need another freeway, there were too many already; but his protests went ignored. Resident pensioners were relocated to a slightly more expensive boarding house in nearby Boyle Heights. Transients were expected to find other housing on their own. Linus had a hundred and nine dollars to his name at the time, a typewriter, a gold watch, some blankets and books, an Olds 88 and his clothes. He hocked the gold watch and moved into his car.

Lily took the money from the sale of the hotel, paid her back taxes, and flew to Florida to live with her ailing sister.

Sometimes Linus drove to Santa Monica and parked near the beach and slept. Other times he parked down a quiet side street in town. The Olds had a long, wide backseat, it wasn't too uncomfortable, but this was winter and it was cold. There was always the fear of harassment, too. Police. Punks. The footsteps of strangers passed at odd hours of the night, and the headlights of moving cars would glance through the cab at all hours of the night no matter where he seemed to park. He'd wake up with his heart racing, the windows white with moisture, and feel for the steak knife that he kept inside his jacket. But three restless nights in a row and he'd pass out on the fourth, which truly scared him. His entire car could be stripped to the frame. He could be murdered and never wake up. For the most part, though, sleeping in the backseat of the Olds was at least tolerable until it began to storm.

One evening Linus stood in the doorway after rehearsals and watched it come down hard and fast, turn into hail and bounce off the sidewalk below. The old man came up from behind and looked over his shoulder.

"Time to lock up," he said.

"Sure."

"Do you want to come downstairs for a while and see if it stops?"

"I better not," he said. "I should get home."

"Suit yourself."

Linus zipped up his jacket and made a dash for the car.

One headlight was out, the windshield wipers were worn, and the defroster was broken. Rain and darkness made the dividing lines almost impossible to see. As he drove hail ticked against the hood, the roof, the windows. Another car suddenly passed him, kicking up a stream of water in its wake. The road melted and blurred and he hit the brakes and they caught and he went into a spin, the rear end sliding one way, the front end another. He braced himself for the crunch of metal, the crack of glass, but the Olds just died in the middle of the street with its windshield wipers slapping back and forth. Linus waited a few seconds for his heart to stop pounding, then he sighed, started it up again and glanced at the gas gauge. The needle rested a fraction above empty. Turning down a side street, he parked, killed the engine and climbed into the back seat.

The blanket he normally used lay on the floorboard, but when he reached for it he found that it was sopping wet. So he threw it back down, tugged his jacket up high around his neck, hunched his shoulders and jammed his hands into his pockets. Once his body generated a circle of warmth, he was afraid to move. Cold vinyl was only an inch away. For several minutes he lay shivering, his eyes wide, watching his breath turn white. Hail continued to tick against the windows and strong winds rocked the car. A drop of water slipped through the ceiling upholstery and landed on his head and then another and another, before he could react, fell on his neck.

"Damn it," he said.

He pushed the corner of one of the wet blankets into the leak and the upholstery bulged, rippled under the weight of the water, then it tore. A gallon or more rushed down on him.

He dove into the front seat and drove back to the theatre. The old man might put him up for the night; he could say he had car trouble, or the truth—that he ran out of gas. The wind caught the door as he opened it and whipped it out of his hand. He forced it shut, then ran through the rain to the porch. The living room drapes were open, he could see it was dark inside, and as he stood there soaked and tired, water running down the back of his neck, he wasn't sure if he should trouble the old man. He felt for his wallet, opened it and counted in the darkness. Forty-two bucks. If he stayed at the Motel Six, it still wouldn't leave him much for gas. He had to find a job, fast. A plastic trash can caught in the wind rolled end over end down the street.

Quietly, though there was no need for it, as the sound of the hail pelting the roof was loud enough to mask his footsteps, he walked around the porch and up the stairs to the theatre. The door was locked but it had an old window in it, four panes set in a removable wood frame. All he had to do was take the steak knife from his jacket and slip it between the crack until he caught the top latch. Then he felt inside for the door knob.

Henry didn't hear him the first night or the second either. But the third night, when the storm had passed, as he lay in bed unable to sleep, a creaking stair gave it away. He put on his bathrobe, grabbed the baseball bat he kept in his closet for just such emergencies and crept to the front door. Opened it. Looked around. No one. He clutched the bat more tightly and walked along the porch to the staircase and peered around the corner. And sure enough, there stood Linus on the landing under the moonlight, with the window frame in hand. Henry ducked out of sight. Down the street, parked at the curb, he spotted the Olds 88.

Come morning the old man went upstairs to inspect the theatre. Nothing was damaged, nothing was missing. The only noticeable difference was with the sofa bed in the dressing room and how the cushions had been plumped and neatly arranged. And so the game continued. Henry heard him come and go, and as he listened to his footsteps on the stairs or the creak of a door as the boy pushed it open, whether it was late at night or in the early morning hours when they both should've been asleep, he wondered if he ought to confront him and if it was the right thing to do. Some way, somehow he always found an excuse to postpone it.

Each night Linus left after rehearsals, parked for a couple of hours, then returned to the theatre. Sometimes, through the living room window, he saw the old man sitting on the couch, reading, as he rode slowly by in the car. Sometimes the blue-gray light from the TV flickered against the wall, sometimes not. Sometimes the drapes were closed and he only saw the old man's twisted shadow move across the room. Hours might pass. It could be one, two in the morning and he'd still be up. Once Linus found himself cursing the old man, because he couldn't slip into the theatre with him still awake and he had to keep circling the block, parking for a while longer, then trying again. But the light had remained on until four that morning. Why couldn't the old fart go to sleep like everybody else? Then he realized that it was his anger talking and that maybe Henry couldn't sleep and that without the theatre and the actors the old man's life wasn't all that different from his own.

Visiting Hour opened to a few students from USC who had seen the flyers Linus posted in the Drama Department, a neighborhood couple, a half dozen others and an aging character actor, a friend of Henry's who had come in drunk and loud. But minutes before the play ended, the students got up and left, and Linus felt like shrugging and doing the same. The distraction was all it took; he was supposed to dim the lights from backstage and enter as Henry shouted for the nurse. His appearance, a silhouette under a single blue flood lamp, marked the finish. But there were a dozen knobs on the control panel and he panicked and forgot which ones to turn. By the time he got it straight he was so flustered he didn't hear the cue. The old man repeated himself more loudly, more urgently when the neighborhood couple and the friend began to clap. It was then that Linus realized the mistake.

A few seconds later he stepped out from behind the curtain.

"Sorry," he whispered, as they did their bows.

"It worked out fine."

"No," he said. "I messed up."

They hurried off stage. Applause grew louder. The friend shouted for Henry.

"C'mon."

"It's for you," Linus said.

The old man took him by the arm anyway and led him back on stage. They did another set of bows.

Afterward Linus quickly changed into his street clothes and slipped past the few people waiting in the theatre. He headed down the stairs as Henry stepped onto the landing with a bottle of champagne tucked under his arm.

"Where you going?"

He stopped. He turned around.

Henry motioned toward the theatre with his chin.

"They want to congratulate you," he said. "Come back up and have a drink."

Linus wanted one, that was for sure, but not wine. Something stronger. Something that burned so you knew what you were drinking.

"I have to get home."

"You mad at me?"

"Why should I be mad?"

"There'll be more people tomorrow," Henry said.

"It always takes a little time."

He shrugged and started down the stairs again when the old man called to him.

"Hey, Eddie. Catch."

He turned. He saw the key falling toward him and snapped it out of the air.

Henry winked.

"Sleep in tomorrow," he said. "I'll have breakfast ready at eight."

5

Withdrawal	Deposit	Balance
———	$ 10.00	$ 4,994.23
———	———	4,994.23
$ 2,075.00	———	2,919.23

He drew his finger down the withdrawal column and stopped. The money had gone to Saint Vincent's when he had his stroke. Medicare paid the bulk of the bill but another illness, a single day in the hospital, or ten minutes on one of their machines would easily wipe him out. Goddamned doctors, goddamned lawyers, too. They bled the old and the poor to death. Henry closed the passbook and poured himself another glass of wine. The letter from the Department of Transportation still rested on the TV tray and he picked it up, crumpled it into a ball and threw it across the room. There was no way in hell he could afford to fight the bastards in court, not that it would've done any good.

They had spoken twice over the phone, he and Jacob Waters, once when he received the first "offer" for his home by registered mail, and another time a few weeks later. In the first conversation the superintendent was polite and led Henry to believe that he sympathized with his plight. What could've easily become an argument ended calmly with Mr. Waters promising to present the grievance at the next board meeting. The second of several letters arrived soon afterward with news that the grievance had been "considered, seriously considered, but our hands are simply tied." Henry phoned him again, except this time Waters wasn't so cordial. Flatly he was told the project could not, and would not, be halted, changed or delayed in any way whatsoever. He would have to move. No exceptions to the rule. Seven other calls to his office died with the secretary.

He sealed the letter he'd written earlier, put a stamp on it, then went for his coat. It lay on top of the television, and as he picked it up he noticed the picture of Evelyn and him perched beside it. She sat on a bed in a motel room, her dress low on her smooth, tanned shoulders, the hem well above her knees, while Henry—much younger back then—kneeled on the floor in front of her. He held her shoe in his hand as she smiled down at him. It wasn't an act, the smile, but he had been in love with another then, Jessica, a costume designer. They had lived together eleven months, here in this same house, and she was the only woman he'd ever thought that he would've wanted to marry. They even set a date, too, but it didn't happen. They ended up quarrelling too much, over the smallest things, especially when they drank, and they both liked to drink too much in those days.

There were others after Jessica, a few before her, but there was no one except Evelyn he cared to remember with any particular fondness. But she was serious with another man by the time he and Jessica parted, and they married later that same year. The man was dead now. Henry wondered if theirs had been a good marriage, if she had been happy, and if she also sometimes wondered what it might've been like had the timing been different. That was the past, though, and he didn't like to think about the past much anymore. He had thrown away all of Jessica's pictures, her near empty bottles of cologne and an old silk robe left in the hamper, a week after she walked out on him, when he knew for certain that she wasn't coming back. He slipped into his coat and headed to the kitchen.

There he opened the drawer where he kept his tools, put a pair of channel-lock pliers into one pocket, a flashlight into another, then opened the cupboard above him. From it he took a two-pound box of sugar, which he hid beneath his coat. Outside he let the screen door close quietly behind him. The night air was warm, dry and still. He drew a deep breath and inhaled the scent of his roses that grew along the front porch. The letter to Jacob Waters, he placed on the rack under his mailbox and started on his way. He wasn't used to walking about at night, usually he stayed home and watched TV or read, and he had to stop and rest every now and then. His knee ached, and though he knew he could've used a cane, if only for the protection, he didn't want to be seen with one. Henry felt for the channel-locks in his pocket and squeezed them. His grip was strong despite the stroke, despite one of those little synapses in his brain gone haywire, that simple pop of a cell, he could make a fist again and hold it for longer than he had in months.

Windows of the houses and apartments were boarded up. Graffiti marred walls and CT, CalTrans' initials, were written in orange spray paint on the side of each building. Some of the homes, already up on blocks, would soon be loaded onto flatbed semis and auctioned to the public. Others, like his own, considered too old and beat up to salvage, would be leveled and hauled away in pieces. Henry continued down the street, glancing over his shoulder every now and then to make sure there was no one behind him. He passed the place where Roy's Market used to be, where he had liked to shop, but there was nothing left of it except the rubble.

He passed the old Royal Hotel. He passed Fanny's Cafe where he used to order the ham-and-egg special on Sunday mornings, and the Thai restaurant that he'd never had a chance to try. He passed McAulay's Shoe store on the corner where he used to have his soles redone. He passed other shops and stores that he used to trade with, now all empty, now all boarded up, until finally he found himself stopped at the chain link fence. Behind it tractors, portable toilets and bulldozers rested—*reposed*, he thought—in the moonlight. Again he glanced over his shoulder, but the streets were deserted. Far in the distance lights glowed in the Trans-American tower downtown.

Somewhere in the darkness he heard the sound of crickets. Henry took a deep breath and approached the main gates, locked loosely together with a shiny new chain. He held them apart and tried to squeeze through, but the metal bars pressed tightly against his chest. He wriggled free then looked up at the fence and wagged his head. There was a time, and not so long ago, when he could have jumped, grabbed the top rail and easily heaved himself over. Now he wasn't sure. Slipping the toe of his shoe into one of the links, Henry reached up as far as he could and took a good hold, then slowly pulled himself off the ground. The fence bowed. The metal cut into his fingers. He arched backward and grunted, eased his foot up, then the other again, and lifted his leg over the top when the fence began to sway. He clung tight and for a moment he thought he had his balance. But his sleeve caught on the sharp edge of an open link and down he went, but not so far, only the last few feet, and then not so hard. The sleeve, as he dropped, tore loose from his coat and broke the worst of the fall. He landed on his ass where he sat for a while, dazed, shaking his head to clear his vision. A bird lost in the night zigzagged through the sky.

Soon Henry picked himself up and flipped on the flashlight. He ran the beam across the yard. There were backhoes. Dozers. An aluminum shed. A grid-roller and the crane with its wrecking ball. His heart beat faster. He followed the light across the yard to the big crane, placed his hands on the tracks, and again, grunting, pulled himself from the ground. The fuel cap was under the cab and he turned it until it clicked into the locked position, then he took the pliers out of his pocket. The bird shrieked. For a moment he froze, he listened, but it was quiet except for the sound of the crickets. Bracing himself, Henry wedged the pliers under the lip of the cap, brought his weight to his shoulders and pushed down hard. The cap flew across the yard and he tumbled backward, catching himself with his good hand straight out. A sharp hot pain shot up his arm to the base of his skull. Immediately his wrist swelled and began to throb and he dropped the flashlight. It fell between the treads of the crane and cracked the lens.

Darkness.

"Oh shit," he said.

He climbed down off the crane, slowly, as best he could with one hand and no light. He hurried back to the fence. But looking up at it, this web, this cage now, he knew that it was impossible to escape. He'd try though. He would try again and again and then he would wag his head and curse himself for a fool. The first thing the demo crew would notice, he thought, come morning when they pulled up in their trucks, was the coat sleeve.

It dangled from the top of the fence like a fucking welcoming banner.

6

Again the neighbor parked his Ferrari half blocking her driveway. She'd give him one more chance and then no more backing up. No more pulling forward. Next time she'd ram the damn thing and pretend she hadn't seen it. Evelyn struggled with the steering wheel, finally worked the transmission into first, and started down the mountain, when a wild-eyed teenager pulled up beside her in the wrong lane. For no reason, except that maybe she drove slowly, he flipped her off, cut in ahead of her and slammed on his brakes. Little bastard, she thought. Get his license. But then he sped off, and what would she do with the number anyway?

Evelyn fumbled through her purse for a cigarette, slipped it between her lips, then took it away. Only the day before the doctor had told her that she had to quit or she could look forward to emphysema in a couple of years, maybe cancer. "Let me show you something," he'd said, in this voice so full of concern that it bordered condescension. That she didn't need. She put the cigarette back in her mouth, lit it and inhaled deeply. The studio bio said she was sixty-one and it was four years too generous, so what was the big deal?

"Look," the doctor had said, "these are your lungs."

Evelyn had shrugged and fought the urge to interrupt, to either get up and leave or to tell him bluntly that she feared all kinds of things but death wasn't one of them, though she hoped that when it came it came quickly. Instead she just sat on the examination table like a good patient, with her hands folded in her lap and her eyes fixed on the X-ray of her rotting lungs. "They should look clear," he'd said, "not black." There was a phone on the wall behind the doctor and she'd thought of Henry when she saw it. She scolded herself for not calling information and getting his number, so she could apologize for that jerk of an A.D. she had to work with, who had turned her friend away. If he'd been protective for a good reason, she might've understood, but he enjoyed what little authority he carried and rarely used it graciously.

The morning traffic was backed up along Franklin. At the bottom of the hill Evelyn stopped and switched on the turn signal. She waited patiently, one foot depressing the clutch, the other on the brake, but no one would let her in, let alone look her in the eye. A minute passed, then another and she rolled down her window, smiled and waved to the driver of a van in front of her. But he just stared directly ahead. When the traffic began to move again Evelyn took her foot off the brake and let the Datsun roll into the street. The van and another car came to a halt. One honked the horn. Evelyn leaned over the wheel and, feigning poor eyesight, pulled into the center of the road. One courtesy deserved another. No one was going anywhere until some kind soul wised up and took heart.

It was seven o'clock when she finally arrived at the

studio, and a little after eight before the make-up man had finished with her and left. Now a thick layer of rouge hid the wrinkles in the corners of her eyes, and her gray hair, which she usually wore down or pinned in a bun, was ratted into a stiff bouffant. Evelyn looked at herself in the full length mirror on the back of the door. This wasn't her, it was some mannequin, some fool in a smart black skirt and matching jacket that fit too tightly. The day had just begun but already she wished it was over.

There was a knock on her door.

"Evelyn?"

"Yeah?"

She answered the door and the A.D. handed her a half dozen pages of script.

"There's been a few changes," he said. "Take your time on them. We won't be needing you for a couple hours."

"Fine."

Just fine, she thought.

No sooner had she shut the door when the trailer suddenly shook. She went to the window and pulled the drapes open. Outside a chauffeur in a white limousine was backing up, pulling forward, trying to turn around in the middle of the driveway. The license plate read OKEEFE.

Again the limousine bumped the trailer.

The first time might've been an accident. But the second? That was simply malicious. Evelyn shook her head, closed the drapes and turned her attention to the script. It was either that or throw open the door and scream at him and she'd already had her fill of dealing with trouble for the day.

INT. OFFICE—EVENING

CLOSE ON MACON

Dead drunk at his desk, when Till enters the office. He slowly raises his head.

TILL
Macon, we're due in court in twenty minutes.

CUT TO:

There were other changes, mostly to the dialogue, but the biggest was directorial. In the earlier draft she entered the office, found Danny passed out and made haste to revive him. A slap or two. It wasn't much. Maybe she had hit him a little harder than necessary, but it made for a good take, it most certainly got the job done mor quickly, and she had to admit that it did feel pretty good. Evelyn smiled. What bothered her wasn't so much that the script had been rewritten, or that most of her lines had been lifted, but that it had all been done solely on Danny's request. He'd gotten his way, and again, from what she could tell, for apparently no legitimate reason.

She tossed the script on the bed and went to the water cooler. For a short while, as she filled a paper cup, she rested her cheek against the cool glass and felt the bubbles inside the bottle rise to the top and burst. Three years on this show, three years of Danny and problems, headaches and boring scripts written by young writers who had been raised on little more than TV and who as talents had burned themselves out before they could know any different. She fumbled inside her purse for her aspirin, uncapped the bottle, shook two out and washed them down with the water.

On the dresser rested the morning paper. She read the headlines. She read a few articles and before she found herself getting depressed she skipped to the local news. Local color. There, on the second page, was a picture of Henry and beneath it the story:

> Crewmen on Project 112, the freeway currently under construction near downtown Los Angeles, had a surprise early yesterday morning when they arrived on the job and found seventy-four year old former character actor Henry Martin trapped inside the equipment yard. Best known for his roles in such films as *Pearl of Blood* and *Doctor X*, Martin is the last remaining resident of the inner city neighborhood scheduled for demo-lition. Mr. Martin, allegedly attempting to sabotage the heavy machinery, injured himself in the process and is now recovering, in good condition, in the Jail Unit of the Los Angeles County Hospital....

Evelyn dropped the paper on the dresser, changed back into her jeans, her blouse, and quickly removed her make-up. As she hurried down the driveway to her car, she saw Danny enter his trailer. The door was marked with a big gold star beneath his name, O'Keefe, and from inside, as Evelyn passed by, she heard a young girl laughing. About what she didn't know, though she could certainly imagine, and the thought alone, without the least sense of prudery, made her squeamish.

*

7

Light from the street lamps passed through the cab of Evelyn's Datsun. The white plaster cast on the old man's arm looked extraordinarily bright against the black interior, as if it had absorbed the flashes of light, as if it were glowing. He leaned back in his seat and looked out the window. Another car passed them with a strong swoosh of air. Henry sighed. This wasn't how he wanted to rekindle an old friendship.

Ahead of them, Linus led the way in his Olds 88. He had been to the hospital twice before already, the first time after Henry called him and told him what had happened. Linus had been furious. "What the hell do you think you were doing? Only a punk kid would act like that," he'd said. "You could've broken your neck. Shit, Henry, you could've killed yourself." But the old man hadn't wanted to hear it. He felt shamed enough already and not so much for what he'd tried to do as that he had failed at it. Now they were stopped at an intersection on Alvarado, the Datsun right behind the Olds, waiting for the light to change.

Evelyn lit a cigarette.

"When do you have to leave?"

"Huh?"

"Your place," she said. "When are you supposed to move?"

"When I'm goddamned good and ready."

She made a clucking noise with her tongue.

Henry cleared his throat.

"Thanks for bailing me out," he said. "I'll write you a check soon as we get back to the house."

The light dropped to green. The Olds took off and Evelyn followed it through the cloud of exhaust left in its wake. They rode the rest of the way in silence. At the house, when they had parked at the curb, he thanked her again and started to climb out of the car. But Evelyn was quick to get out before him, walk around and open his door.

The cab light flashed on and he saw Linus standing beside her. He waved them back.

"I can do it myself," he said. "Does it look like I broke my legs too?"

Evelyn glanced at Linus.

"Is he always this mean?" she said.

Linus just shrugged.

They followed Henry up to the front door, where he felt inside his pocket for his keys. He stabbed one at the lock. But it was dark, he couldn't see well and the key wouldn't fit.

"You're standing in my light," he said. "Move out of the way."

He held the key up to the moon to make sure he had the right one, and that he had it the right side up and then he tried it again. This time it worked. He pushed open the door, he switched on the light and stood away. Evelyn slipped by him.

"It's a little messy," he said. "I've been too busy to clean."

"Can I use your bathroom?"

"Down the hall," he said. "The last door on your right."

When she'd gone, when he heard her close the door,

he turned to Linus. The kid was staring at him.

"What're you looking at?"

"Sometimes," he said. "Sometimes I just can't believe you, man."

"That's enough now."

Linus wagged his head.

"You have to admit," he said, "it really was a stupid thing to do."

Henry raised his voice. "I told you," he said, "I don't want to hear it. Run get my checkbook. It's on the dresser in my room."

Bail had been set at five thousand dollars, which meant that he had to write Evelyn a check for five hundred to cover what she'd given the bondsman. The hearing was supposed to be held within thirty days, when he would be formally charged with trespassing, vandalism—two misdemeanors—and attempted destruction of state property, a felony that carried with it a considerable fine. The thought of going to court, pleading his case and losing as he was certain he would, and then trying to come up with money that he didn't have both scared and disgusted him. But he wasn't about to let the kid or Evelyn know that. What he needed now was a shot of whiskey, two or three of them, back to back.

Linus returned with the checkbook and the old man wrote one out and tried to hand it to Evelyn when she came back into the kitchen. She smelled of fresh rose water.

"Forget it." She waved the check away. "It's on me. If there's one thing I have, it's plenty of money."

"No," he said. "That's not the way I like to do business."

"Business?" she said. "This isn't business, Henry. I

didn't bail you out because of your good looks."

That got a smile out of him. But he was still determined to have his way. Evelyn had set her purse on the kitchen table when they first came in, and he slipped the check inside it.

"There," he said. "End of argument."

"We're putting on a play I wrote," Linus said.

Henry glared at him.

"Hush now."

"Where?" Evelyn said.

"Here," Linus said. "Henry built a little theatre upstairs."

"Really?" she said.

"It isn't much," Henry said. "But it keeps me and the boy busy." At that he took Evelyn by the arm and walked her to the door.

"I'm sure you got plenty to do," he said, "but maybe we could get together for lunch sometime. Remember the Brown Derby?"

"Of course," she said. "But you know they tore it down."

"No."

"Wil Wright's, too. That's gone. And Schwab's. Leveled," she said. "To the ground. They put in a mini-mall."

"Christ, what's next?"

"This place," Linus said.

Henry shot him a look off the shoulder.

"Over my dead body," he said.

He and Evelyn stepped to the porch.

"Anyway," she said, "about lunch. I'd like that."

They wrote each other's addresses and phone numbers on slips of paper and then she gave him a good long hug and walked to her car. He waited there on the porch until her Datsun had disappeared down the street before he sighed, turned and went back inside. Linus was leaning against the kitchen counter with his arms crossed over his chest.

"Well?" he said.

"Well what?"

"Is she going to do it?"

Henry took a long, deep breath.

"Listen," he said, "she bailed me out tonight. She drove me home. Think about it, Eddie. Think. Then you tell me how I could ask if she wants to work in a little play with a couple has-beens?"

Linus pushed himself away from the counter.

"I'm not a fucking has-been."

Then he was gone, out the door, slamming it behind him.

Another night Henry might've followed, he might've tried to doctor the wound, but he was worn out and all he wanted now was sleep. He'd been awake for nearly forty-eight hours. He wandered down the hall to his room, flipped on the light and emptied his coat pockets onto the dresser. Keys. A roll of Tums. Two nickels and a dime.

"Damn," he muttered.

In her hand was the check for five hundred dollars.

There was no one to tailgate her. There was no one ahead. It was just empty road, winding up, curving now and then. Imagine, she thought, if it were always like this. Quiet. No pressures ahead or behind. At the top of the mountain she took her foot off the accelerator for a moment and looked out over the valley. On a clear night she could see past Hollywood, the skyscrapers and all the lights across the valley to the dark expanse of the Pacific in the distance. On those days when there was a good breeze, and the sun was shining, the town below reminded her of the old Hollywood, the one that she liked to remember. Tall, shaggy palm trees and studios. Spanish bungalows. The wide streets used to be free of the litter and traffic, so clean the concrete shone white in the glare of the morning sun. But tonight the sky was smoggy and she couldn't see beyond the Pacific Theatre tower.

Evelyn took the transmission out of gear and coasted down the road, around a sharp bend and into her driveway at the end of a cul-de-sac. Large showcase houses made of stucco and glass bordered her home, which was tucked back a ways off the street, and hidden behind a tangle of overgrown bushes and shrubs. She turned off the ignition and stepped out of the car and headed down a dark narrow path scattered with leaves and gnarled branches. She and her husband used to rake the falling and stuff it into plastic bags. The day that Les died she'd been planting violets along the side of the house where the most sun fell.

He'd been on the ladder in the front yard, pruning the lemon tree. The dark soil tumbled beneath the spade as Evelyn stabbed it into the earth, lifted and turned. Carefully she removed the flowers from the cartons and placed them into the holes she dug, one by one, pressing the earth down firmly around them with her palms. Then she stood back to admire her work: the row of violets, the row of purples and yellows, perfectly straight. She slapped the dirt off her hands and went to get Les because she was proud of her work and wanted to show him. But he lay on a pile of freshly cut lemon branches, his lips pale blue and the shears still in his hand. Later the doctor told her that it was a massive coronary, and from that day on she stopped spending her weekends working around the yard except to water.

Since then eleven years had passed and the plants had continued to grow unchecked, uncut. Last summer her neighbor volunteered his gardener, but Evelyn had come to like the privacy, that sense of enclosure the vines and the trees afforded. No, she'd told him. Thank you but no. Ivy clung to the walls of her house, wrapped around the porch posts and crept beneath the wooden shingles of the roof. Dry leaves crackled under her feet. She let herself into the house and saw, as she entered, the red light of her answering machine blinking on and off in the darkness.

She went to the kitchen, made herself a drink, then returned to the living room and pressed the rewind button. The tape spun, then made a clicking noise. It was her agent.

> *Evelyn, give me a call when you get home. I think you know what it's about.*

There was a pause, a hum, another message.

> *This is Larry, babe. Why'd you walk out on us? Let's talk. I don't care what time you get in, just call me.*

She hit the off-button and then picked up her purse and rummaged through it. When she found the slip of paper, she reached for the phone and dialed. As she listened to it ring she wondered if it wasn't too late, if maybe she ought to hang up, but a moment later he answered.

His voice sounded groggy.

"Hello?"

"Henry?"

"Who's this?"

"Evelyn. Did I wake you?"

"It's okay," he said. "Is something wrong?"

She took a sip of her drink. Whiskey on ice.

"That play you're doing," she said. "Is there a role in it for me? It's been a long time since we worked together, Henry."

8

Thirty feet of broken lights and bent iron lay partially dismantled on the rooftop of an old building across from the Royal Hotel. It was the framework of a marquee from a bygone era. Executives of the investment firm that bought the place were told by the remodeling contractor that it was cheaper to leave the old sign on the roof than to break it down and haul it off. In its place they installed a new, modern one that flashed *Adult Books & Movies* in red neon over the yellow, plastic silhouette of a nude woman. A few years later, when the City of L.A. announced plans for Project 115, the investment firm closed the theatre doors and bailed out at a healthy profit. Left behind was the old marquee.

Worn through storm and time, only the elderly residents of the Royal Hotel, and only those who had rooms on the upper floors that looked down on the sign, knew what the rusting and bent letters had once spelled. Although Henry had never lived in the Royal, he'd been out walking, just a stroll before breakfast to build an appetite, the day the workmen cracked the mounts. For hours he'd watched them from the curb across the street, listening to the crunch of metal and the hiss of blowtorches, waiting for the scraps to be lowered to the ground. Instead a big truck with a crane pulled up and the men raised the new sign and fastened it into place. The original, too worthless to dismantle, had been left to rust. The Lightning Palace was what it had once read.

All lit up, it could be seen for miles. It was the first sign that Henry had spotted, that had made his heart pound, as he stood at the open door of a Southern Pacific boxcar rumbling through Los Angeles in the dead of night. He was seventeen then and a thousand miles from his hometown of Portland, Oregon. The earth moved fast beneath him. The pulse and clatter of steel wheels and couplings vibrated up through the soles of his shoes, through his legs, to his chest, and he could smell the hot smoking axle grease. He tossed his blanket roll, bent his knees and jumped. Wind struck him, then he hit ground. Gravel bit into his hands and arms and ripped his pants at the knee. The train rumbled on until the earth was again still and silent. Henry picked himself up, found his bed roll a good fifty yards from where he'd landed, slung it over his shoulder and started for the lights of the marquee.

The box office was closed for the night and the streets were deserted.

The Golden Apple
Starring

Clayton Burrows
Alister Canning
Jennifer Lockard

Someday, instead of Burrows holding the beautiful Jennifer Lockard in his arms, it would be Henry—star of moving pictures and theatre. This was the big time, this was the place, this Los Angeles. City of stars. Perfect weather. Gorgeous women. Henry shut his eyes and imagined himself on the huge silver screen. The applause, when the curtains closed, sounded like thunder, but that memory had long given way to the roar of the demolition crews and the big break never came. His career had been cut short by the House Un-American Activities Committee when he was subpoenaed to testify against the D.P. on *Doctor X* and chose instead to take the Fifth. He was thirty-eight years old at the time and steadily working toward roles that might have one day made him a star. Maybe. Maybe not. But as the years had continued to pass, one into another, without shape or design, the recognition that he'd once thought inevitable had given way to a silence as impenetrable as his own vow.

Now as Henry lay in bed, the cast on his arm heavy at his side, he could hear them advancing again, still closer. It was morning and the whine of the engines seemed louder than usual, the fall of the wreckage more intense. He sat up in bed and reached for the copy of the play on the nightstand, opened it and read.

THE ROYAL HOTEL

by Edward Shapiro

A top story room in a decaying hotel in downtown Los Angeles. The window overlooks the street below. One door leads to the bathroom; another, center stage, exits into a dark hallway. An elevator door can be seen in the background when the center stage door is opened.

The distant sound of diesel engines and the crash of wreckage is heard as the lights rise, revealing GARY LOMBARDO, standing at the window. It's morning and he's dressed in a shabby bathrobe. LILY HILL enters, carrying a breakfast tray. She looks like she's had a rough night.

LILY: The last tenant packed up and left this morning. It's just you, me and Bert now.

GARY: Cowards.

LILY: Who?

GARY: The tenants.

Lily goes to the table and puts down the breakfast tray. On it are four glasses of juice and a plate of mixed grains. As she transfers the glasses from the tray to the table, she says:

LILY: Apricot juice. Nectarine juice. Carrot juice. Orange juice.

Gary approaches and looks at the plate of mixed grains.

GARY: What's this?

LILY: Barley. Oats. Bran. It's to clean out your system.

GARY: It's clean already.

LILY: Just eat it, please. I made it special for you.

Gary returns to the window. He motions for Lily to follow. She obeys, although reluctantly.

GARY: Take a look?

She does.

GARY: What'd you see?

LILY: Rooftops, streets, smog.

He lifts the window open and the roar of the machinery grows louder.

GARY: Lean out. Look again. (A beat, as she obeys.) What do you see now?

LILY: The crew, the crew and the tractors.

GARY: Farther.

LILY: Nothing. It's all gone. Gary, I don't feel like playing games.

GARY: Look at the theatre. In the doorway. See him? The fat man?

LILY: Please, Gary.

GARY: Jesus, are you blind?

Lily finally gives in.

LILY: I see him. Of course.

GARY: He's older, he's fatter, but it's him. I can smell the rot from here.

Lily shuts the window and takes Gary by the hand.

LILY: Eat your breakfast, please. You need your strength.

There was a knock on the front door. Henry set the script down, put on his bathrobe and went to answer it. But he was slow in getting there and whoever it was knocked again, louder this time—an impatient rap.

"Mr. Martin?"

The voice didn't belong to anyone he knew.

Henry stopped in the living room. The drapes were drawn and no one could see in.

"I know you're there," the voice said. "Answer the door."

But he didn't move, didn't speak.

"I have a message for you from Mr. Waters."

Pause.

"You listening?"

More silence.

"We intend to press charges, Mr. Martin. And we're talking a felony offense here," he said. "Seems to me it'd be in your best interests to give Mr. Waters a call. We might be able to work something out."

Seconds later he heard him skip down the stairs, then the scuffle of his shoes on the sidewalk. That sound was followed by the roar of an engine, and when it too had faded Henry went to the window and parted the curtains. A state-issued Plymouth made its way down the street. He let the curtains fall back into place and went to the kitchen where he picked up the phone and, with his good hand, dialed. A secretary answered.

"Department of Transportation."

"Let me speak to Waters."

"May I ask who's calling?"

"Martin," he said. "Henry Martin."

"One moment please."

Jacob Waters came on the line.

"What can I do for you, Mr. Martin?"

Henry cradled the receiver, chin to shoulder. His voice trembled, though he didn't know why. It had nothing to do with fear, and as far as anger was concerned he'd learned to mask that well enough.

"Your henchman was just here."

"I wouldn't exactly call him that."

"Same by any name," he said. "You can take your charges, Mr. Water. You can take them and press them right up your ass."

There was a moment of stunned silence on the other end. Then the line went dead. Henry hung up and grabbed a broom from behind the refrigerator and used the blunt end to pound on the ceiling. The dressing room was directly above him.

"Wake up," he shouted.

He pounded again.

"Wake up. I have some good news."

Soon Linus appeared at the front door, barefoot and sleepy eyed, with his t-shirt untucked and his hair mussed.

"Who was that guy?" he said.

"What guy?"

"The guy I heard shouting."

"Nobody," Henry said.

"So what's this?"

Linus nodded at the door. There was a red sheet of paper taped to it and in big bold black letters it read *Eviction*. Henry stepped past him.

"Paper," he said, as he ripped it down. "Nothing but a lousy piece of paper." He crumpled it into a ball, took aim at the wastebasket and let it sail.

Two points.

"Now," he said, "about that good news."

The Olds 88 bogged down on the incline into the

Hollywood Hills. They crawled up the mountain in low gear until they came to a fork in the road across from a Japanese restaurant that overlooked the city. On the seat between them rested a fresh copy of the *Royal Hotel*. They'd had it made at Charlie Chan's earlier that same morning.

"Which way now?"

"Stay to your right," Henry said.

Linus looked at the temperature gauge on the dash, for the Olds tended to overheat on hills, and his worry was confirmed. The needle was edging slowly into the red. He flipped on the radio, hoping they would reach the peak soon and that the engine would have a chance to cool. Scratchy sounding rock-and-roll filled the cab. Henry winced, reached over and turned off the radio.

"Just concentrate on the road," he said, "and keep your eyes peeled. We want Ashland."

"You know," Linus said. "I really don't see the point of all this anymore. I mean you can't ignore an eviction notice."

"Sounds like you're scared."

"That has nothing to do with it."

"Any time you want," he said, "you can pack up and go. I ain't stopping you."

"You're missing the point."

"No," he said, "*you're* missing it. They want me, they'll have to drag me out."

"Maybe they'll just level the place with you in it."

"Maybe," he said. "But at least I won't go down a coward."

Henry fumbled through his coat pocket for his cigarettes, found the pack and shook one out. Linus pressed in the lighter for him and sighed. He didn't know what to think. He didn't know what to do. One thing was clear, though: whatever Henry decided, he'd back him up anyway he could. The old man had helped him out plenty of times; he'd given him a place to stay, even acted as a kind of father to him. And consider this, he thought: you're the one who wrote the play in the first place and got him started on the idea of producing it. Now it seemed to Linus that the play was just another complication in the old man's already too complicated life. They would arrest Henry. They could jail him if they wanted, and they just might. Of that much Linus could be certain.

He wasn't paying attention to his driving, so that when another car, a Mercedes, approached he didn't notice it until the last second.

"Turn," Henry shouted.

Linus panicked, pulled hard on the wheel, locked the brakes. The Olds smacked up against the curb, popped over it and skidded to a stop a few feet from the edge of the mountain. Henry looked out the window and sucked in his breath.

"Almost," he said, "almost got us killed again, Eddie."

"There's a railing there."

"They snap," he said. "It doesn't take much."

"Gimme a break."

Henry wagged his head.

"How you ever got your license, I'll never know," he said. "But then they give them out to anybody nowadays."

Linus slammed his palms against the wheel.

"You want to drive?" he said. "Drive."

He threw open the door, slammed it shut and walked around to the other side and got back in. Henry positioned himself behind the wheel and stubbed his cigarette out in the ashtray.

"This is a dangerous old mountain," he said. "You can't be too careful."

He put the transmission into gear, leaned far over the wheel, looked both ways, then let his foot off the brake and eased the car back into the road. Every few seconds, before they rounded one of the blind curves, he tapped the horn. "That's to alert the other driver," he said. "That's what you're *supposed* to do. Watch and learn. I've never been in a wreck in my life and I don't plan on getting in one today, or going over the cliff for that matter." He tapped the horn again, as if to show him how it was done. Linus only glared at him.

In a short while they were stopped at a red light at the bottom of the mountain. Henry blinked.

"We must've passed it," he said.

"Why don't we just go back?"

"You want to know something?"

"No."

"You got a rotten attitude."

"Face it, we're lost."

Henry didn't say anything.

The light dropped to green and he slowly edged the nose of the Olds into the right-hand lane. Linus fastened his seat belt and glanced at the speedometer. They were rolling along at twenty miles-an-hour.

"Think you could go a little slower?"

"If you kept your eyes open as much as you talk," Henry said, "we would've been there already."

"Yeah, right."

It was a small street that fed into a major one and soon there were lots of cars piled up behind them. Ahead, riding near the curb, was a kid on an old ten-speed.

Henry hit the brakes and slowed down.

"You have room," Linus said. "Go around him."

"We have to turn soon."

"Not for three more blocks."

"They'll be on us in no time," Henry said. "We'd just have to get back in this lane anyway."

They followed a few yards behind the bike, and every now and then the kid glanced over his shoulder at them.

"You're making him nervous," Linus said.

But Henry ignored him.

The moment the other drivers behind them had the opportunity, they veered into the left lane and passed. Linus slouched down in his seat while Henry, hunching still further over the wheel, stared straight ahead. In his eyes was the determined look of a man with only one thing on his mind—driving. A minute later they made their turn and were headed back up the mountain. This time around, however, they spotted Ashland Street.

"Don't know where I'm going, huh?" Henry said.

He pulled to the curb behind a red Ferrari, shut off the engine and reached for the play on the seat between them.

"Be back in a second," he said. "I'll just put it on her doorstep."

From the window of a big house, while he waited for Henry to return, he noticed a woman staring at him. Their eyes met briefly, and he wondered what she was thinking about this old beat-up car in her neighborhood. Hoods? Burglars? He heard a hissing noise and looked away from the window. Steam rose from under the hood. Linus climbed out, popped the latch and lifted it open. More steam, a hot wall of it, sent him backwards. The radiator sizzled. Rusty water drained from the overflow tube and into the gutter. He looked up at the window of the big house. Now there was a man staring at him. Linus pointed to the steaming radiator, smiled, and called out.

"Got a rag?"

But the man just shut the drapes. Linus plopped himself down at the curb and looked up at the sky. It was the color of the rusty water rolling past his worn out tennis shoes, around them and into the gutter.

From a window at Spago she studied an electronic billboard across the street. The New Chevrolet. It was dark out now, and every few seconds the door of a huge cardboard Corvette opened and closed, lights flashed, the hood rose, and the tires spun in place. On the street below a stretch limousine cruised by.

"Are you listening to me?"

She nodded, looked away from the window and opened her menu. Across from her sat Larry, the Assistant Director. He had on a satin baseball jacket with *Testimony* embroidered on the back. Underneath it he wore a Hawaiian shirt unbuttoned at the throat. "I think you owe Danny an apology," he said.

"You got it backwards," she said.

"Be reasonable," he said. "I'm trying to patch things up. He's still pushed out of shape about the slap."

Maybe she'd order the filet mignon. But then the pizza sounded good, too. She put the menu down and picked up her drink. The glass was cold to the touch, sweating. At the table across from them sat Karen West in a black dress cut low in the front and a string of pearls around her neck. There wasn't more than a year or two difference in their ages, and they used to be up for many of the same roles. But West looked better than her now, time had been kinder—no bags under her eyes and few if any wrinkles—yet Evelyn took pleasure in knowing that the woman couldn't act her way through a one-liner if her life depended on it.

"I heard David talked with your agent again," he said. "You can't just walk off the lot without costing a lot of people plenty of trouble and money." He rested his elbows on the edge of the table and leaned in. His voice dropped to a whisper. "This is just between me and you. I don't want it going any further. But there's been talk. Evelyn," he said, "it doesn't matter how good of an actress you are."

"Actor."

"What?"

"The term actress," she said, "I hate it. Too much starlet baggage."

"Actor. Actress. I didn't invite you out to argue about words." He held his thumb and index finger about an inch apart. "You're this close, this close to...."

"Spare me," she said. "Because I honestly don't care."

He leaned back in his chair.

"Another round before dinner?"

"You go ahead," she said. "I've had my limit."

She grabbed her purse and made her way past the other tables. But Larry didn't make a move.

On the doorstep she found the script, picked it up and let herself inside the house. She made another drink and then curled up on the couch, turned on the table lamp and began to read. Her eyes burned, she was tired, but she didn't look up from the play until she'd finished it. It was a quirky story, silly in places and sad in others and it brought back both good and bad memories. She wondered how Henry had taken to it, and if Eddie was aware of what he'd touched on. She thought of Henry, of one of the last times they'd seen each other, years back at the commissary at Universal. His hair then had only begun to grey on the sides. He sat alone at a table, dressed in a telegraph operator's outfit from the 1800's. A vest. A pin-striped shirt. An accountant's visor on his head. He had a small role in a TV movie-of-the-week. More of a walk on, he'd said, than anything else—a favor for a friend. She'd been looping for *A Season in Time,* which opened some months later in Westwood to good reviews and big box office. But she hadn't told him exactly what she was there for when he asked. Her success, she'd thought, would only remind him of his past and the witch hunts.

He was a fine actor, and still is, she thought—too fine, anyway, to have gone this long without recognition, without recovering. Instead, when he had asked her what she was doing at the studio that afternoon, she told him that she was just visiting a friend. But it was no one special, no one that he knew. Now, as Evelyn raised the drink to her lips, she imagined herself in the role of Lily, performing on stage with Henry.

When was the last time she'd acted with someone worth a damn? When was the last time she'd really enjoyed it?

She shook her head.

It had been longer, much longer than she cared to remember.

9

Over the distant roar of the machinery, and the crash of the wreckage that followed, Henry and Linus worked side by side in the theatre. They stained plywood the color of dark walnut and decorated it with molding to make for the set walls. They hung an old door that led off stage and opened up to what looked like the front bars of an elevator, but which were only wooden dowels painted black. They cut a window into another stage wall, they swept the aisles and mopped the floors. In the evenings, when Evelyn arrived after work, they rehearsed—first cold, with scripts in hand, sorting out the mechanics of moving about the stage, picking up cues and defining their separate characters—then later, without the script, going through it scene by scene.

A week passed, and Linus designed a flyer:

The Long Awaited Stage Appearance of

EVELYN RICHARDSON

IN

The Royal Hotel

A Musee Imaginaire in Two Acts by

EDWARD SHAPIRO

In Honor of the Demise of a
Historical Los Angeles Landmark

Also Starring
HENRY MARTIN and EDDIE SHAPIRO

AT

The Second Story Theatre, 421 Norwell Street

OPENING NIGHT
June 26, 8:00 PM

Call 555-1542 for Reservations

They rehearsed four nights a week. Henry directed Evelyn, Evelyn directed Henry, and they both directed Linus. Sometimes they played it straight through several scenes, sometimes they skipped ahead to the second act, or backward to the middle of the first act, while other times they played it line by line from the beginning. Often the scene involved only Lily and Lombardo, and Linus would take a seat in the front row of the theatre, bring his knees up to his chest, wrap his arms around his legs and watch.

Toward the end of the second act Lombardo could no longer eat or drink and he barely had the strength to walk. From the window he could see the IRS man on the street below, who by this point had grown so fat that he could hardly stand under his own immense weight. Lily loved the dying man; Linus could see it, feel it in her eyes and in the tender way she rested her hand on his shoulder. Dialogue that Linus had once winced reading aloud to himself, because it sounded false or melodramatic, seemed real and true when Henry and Evelyn acted it out. He'd watched her show before and had always thought that she was good in it, yet he'd never seen her give to the program what she now gave to his play. And Henry, when he raised his voice weakened from hunger and sickness, and looked out the window at his past below, you knew that he saw the fat man consuming him, consuming everything around them.

Things couldn't have seemed better.

Then about a week before opening night, Henry invited them out to dinner at Clifton's Cafeteria. They piled into the front seat of the Olds and made their way out of the condemned neighborhood down North Broadway past Little Tokyo. On the way Linus pulled to the curb, put the transmission into neutral and reached under the seat. He grabbed a couple of flyers off the pile that he kept stashed there, his staple gun, too, and slipped out from behind the wheel.

"This'll just take a second," he said.

He tacked them to a telephone pole and hopped back in the car.

They drove on.

"You really need to do that?" Evelyn said. "Isn't it illegal?"

"Posting flyers?"

"Yes."

"I don't know," Henry said.

"Aren't you supposed to get a permit?" she said. "A license or something?"

"I never heard of such a thing."

"Me, either," Linus said.

He had posted flyers on the USC campus, on telephone poles all over town, he had stuck them under windshield wipers of parked cars in Westwood and West Los Angeles, he'd tacked them over other older posters and flyers wherever he spotted them.

"There's better ways to advertise," she said.

Henry wagged his head.

"You keep your money," he said. "We'll do just fine without it."

On the street outside Clifton's, when they climbed out of the car, Evelyn slipped her arm around Henry's waist. He put his good arm over her shoulder. Walking was awkward with one arm in a cast, but he did his best to keep rhythm with her steps. Her shoulders felt sturdy and strong and warm and he leaned into her and thought to himself that he could've walked for a long time like this. But downtown wasn't what it used to be. The streets seemed dirty, there were more people, and if he had wanted to talk he would've had to shout over the noise from the traffic, all the horns, the passing buses and trucks.

Outside Clifton's two evangelists carried on, both with opened Bibles in hand, as if they were in competition for the attention of the crowds that swarmed past them. Linus ducked between the two men and opened the door for Henry and Evelyn. Inside the cafeteria it was like a movie set; there were three floors and each had a different decor: Wild West, Stone Age and Baroque. They took their trays and got in line.

"Get anything you want," he told them. "This is on me."

Evelyn chose the chipped beef, Linus the Salisbury steak, and for himself it was tuna casserole with a bowl of soup. They decided on a table in the Stone Age, and to get there they had to climb a winding staircase, narrow as a goat's path, lined knee-high by papier-mache rock. On the other side of the mountain was a waterfall.

It had embarrassed Henry, when they had passed by the evangelists on the way in. Evelyn hadn't seemed to mind but he did, knowing that she'd ignored them as much for his sake as her own, so as not to upset him—Henry—the old fool who never got out of the house, who didn't even know a good inexpensive restaurant to take a lady to dinner anymore. But where else? Spending big cash on a meal when you could get the same for less was sinful, he thought. Highway robbery. And on a pension who could afford the places in Westwood, West Los Angeles and Beverly Hills? He couldn't anyway, not anymore, not like he once could when he was pulling in decent wages. Besides, he liked it here. The food wasn't bad, you waited on yourself, and he hadn't forgotten that years before, during the Great Depression, it was Clifton's that had provided free meals to those in need. He wondered, given the times, if they were doing it again.

He smiled at Evelyn.

"How's that chipped beef?" he said.

It was plain, cooked without spices, with a white sauce poured over rice.

"Mmmmm," she said. "Delicious."

"My mother used to take me here when I was a little kid," Linus said, "when we lived in the old Royal. She loved it, but it wasn't because of the food."

Henry gave him a cold look.

"What's that supposed to mean?"

"She just liked the movie set stuff."

"I need to make a quick phone call," Evelyn said. "Where is it around here?"

"Downstairs."

"I'll show you," Henry said. "I have to use the bathroom myself."

They headed back down the goat's path, and when Henry disappeared into the men's room, Evelyn searched through her purse, found a quarter, dropped it into the slot and dialed.

"Century Management."

"Is Cyrus in?"

"One moment, Ms. Richardson."

Cyrus answered a second later.

"What's up, Evelyn?"

"A couple of friends and myself are putting on a play," she said, "and I need some help getting the word out."

"Another charity benefit?"

"Not exactly."

"It really isn't your job to advertise."

"That's my business," she said, "not yours. Do you have a pen?"

She gave him all the necessary information, then hung up and went back to the table. For a while she and Linus talked about the play and picked at their food, trying to eat slowly so they wouldn't finish before Henry returned. A good five minutes must've passed.

"What's taking him?"

Linus shrugged.

"Maybe you better check."

He wiped his mouth with the edge of his napkin and headed down to the main floor, past the pastry counter up front, past the phone and down another set of stairs to the men's room in the basement. He pushed open the door and stepped inside. The fluorescent light above the washbasin flickered and hummed. In the ceiling an exhaust fan with a bad bearing made a grinding noise. From under the stall he saw Henry's baggy pants wadded around his ankles.

"Hey," he said, "you plan on spending your life in here or what? C'mon. We're out there waiting on you, man."

"Eddie?"

The voice was frail, shaky.

"Eddie?"

Suddenly Linus felt faint, his throat swelled, and he took hold of the washbasin to steady himself. Water dripped silently from the faucet.

"I can't move my leg. I can't even get up off the damn toilet. Like a baby," he said. "A *baby*." Slowly Linus pushed the stall door open. The old man stared up at him.

"Eddie," he said. "Eddie, I'm scared. Help me get my goddamn pants back on."

10

When Linus was seven years old his mother entered him in the Big Bonanza Talent Search. The entry fee was only a few dollars and the contestants, according to the ad in *Daily Variety*, would be judged by major talent scouts and casting agents. What could they lose? she thought, tearing the ad from the page. If nothing else her boy would get exposure, maybe a good contact. It was certainly worth a try. Grand Prize was a paid guest appearance on *The Ed Sullivan Show* and runners-up would receive a contract for representation with the Broom Artists Agency in Beverly Hills. Just saying those names, silently—*Beverly Hills, Ed Sullivan, Artists Agency*—conjured up images of high life and glamour. When you lived in Los Angeles the dream seemed so much more real, so much more possible. All you had to do was hustle. All you had to do was want it bad enough and you'd get it. Mrs. Shapiro smiled to herself. Her friends back in San Diego would be impressed.

"Honey?" she called, from over her shoulder.

"Yeah, Mom?"

"C'mere, baby."

He climbed up off the bedroom floor where he'd been kneeling shooting marbles. In the kitchen he found his mother sitting at the table. By the way she smiled at him, her head tilted slightly to one side, and down a little, so she was looking up at him from an angle, he knew immediately that something was up. She slipped her arm around his waist.

"You're going to be in a contest." She pulled him closer, so that they were eye to eye. "You want to be in a contest, honey?"

"What for?"

"To win, silly."

Linus shrugged.

"I guess," he said.

"What do you mean, you guess?"

He stared down at his feet.

"I mean I guess I do."

"It's this Saturday."

It was a Monday, when she came across the ad, and that afternoon they hopped on the bus and rode downtown to Fifth and Broadway. First stop was the barber shop. Linus balked at the door beside the revolving barber's pole. His mother had told him that they were only going shopping. She patted him on the ass, edging him forward.

"C'mon," she said. "Be a big boy."

"I had a haircut last week."

"Don't make a scene."

She grabbed him by the scruff of his neck and led him inside. Up into the chair he went, down around him came the white sheet. He dug his fingernails into the leather armrests.

"Give him a flat top," Mrs. Shapiro said. "Like they do in the Navy."

When Linus heard the shrill buzz of the electric clippers, and saw his soft brown hair tumble in clumps into his lap, his eyes swelled with tears.

"Hey, hey," the barber said. "It isn't that bad. It grows back."

But it was that bad. He didn't need another haircut, he didn't care about the Big Bonanza. He wanted to shoot marbles, read comic books and ride the elevator with Bert Goodman.

Later they went to lunch at Clifton's Cafeteria and then they crossed the street to the Broadway department store. There Mrs. Shapiro had him try on a miniature sailor's uniform. A perfect fit, she thought, as she arranged him in front of the full-length mirror.

"Put your hands on your hips," she said. "Spread your feet a little."

He obeyed.

She adjusted the white cap on his head and stepped back again to look at him.

"Now smile," she said.

He smiled.

Adorable, she thought, just adorable. Maybe his father might not have thought so, as he was army through and through, but then of course he wasn't here. She nodded to herself.

"Bigger," she said. "Give me a big big smile."

He gave her one and she returned it.

"How about a salute?"

Again he obeyed.

Mrs. Shapiro imagined the sour expression that would undoubtedly come over her ex-husband's face if he could just see their boy now. The thought amused her. Maybe she ought to snap his picture and send it to him.

She waved down the clerk.

"We'll take it," she said.

From there they went to the women's department where Linus sat patiently on the couch in the far corner of the room, his suit in a bag beside him, while his mother tried on dress after dress. She wanted something low-cut in the front, something with sheer fabric that clung to her hips, that complimented the fine angles of her body. Finally she found just the one, paid for it, and they caught the bus home.

At the hotel Linus headed straight for the bedroom to pick up where he'd left off playing marbles. But his mother called to him before he could slip out of sight. He stopped in the hallway.

She stood in the kitchen.

"We only have five days to practice," she said. "Get your taps on."

"Mom...."

"You want to win, don't you?"

Mrs. Shapiro pushed the kitchen table against the wall.

"Hurry up," she said.

Then she began to stack the chairs on top of one another, clearing the space, making more room so her son could dance on the hard linoleum floor.

There were jugglers and dancers. There were ventriloquists with their floppy dummies, a tumbling team in tights, actors, musicians, a man with a half dozen white poodles on leashes, and maybe fifty other hopefuls far behind them down the block. Mrs. Shapiro adjusted the strap of her purse on her shoulder and faced forward in the line. Only nine others stood ahead of them. She had counted twice.

"Didn't I tell you?" she said. "Now aren't you glad

we got here early?"

She had roused him out of bed and into the shower at four-thirty that morning, dressed him and polished his shoes. By five he had stood for final inspection in front of the dresser mirror. His mother tugged here and there on his suit, picked a white thread from the dark blue pants and fluffed his flat-top with her palm. "Aren't you excited?" she said. But Linus said nothing. On the bus into town he stared silently out the window, his eyes half-mast, and watched the passing street lamps go out minutes before the sky grew light. By a quarter-to-seven they were standing in line in Hollywood outside Paramount.

Now Linus's feet ached. He shifted his weight from one leg to the other.

"What time is it?" he said.

She started to look at her watch, then let her arm drop back to her side. "I told you five minutes ago," she said. "It's not going to go by any faster you asking."

Linus tried to slip his hands into his pockets, as he had twice before in the last hour, when he remembered the pants didn't have front pockets. And what kind of pants had no front pockets?

He kicked at the sidewalk.

"Stop it," Mrs. Shapiro said. "Those shoes cost money, you know." She grabbed his arm and pulled him back a step. The man ahead of them looked undesirable to her. He wore a tattered coat, he was unshaven and smelled faintly of bourbon, and he carried a beat-up violin case under his arm. She wondered just how long his audition would last, as certainly there had to be standards, even for an open competition.

"Quit wiggling around now," she said. "Straighten up. They'll be opening the doors soon. I just hope you're ready."

"I think so," he mumbled.

"You have to do better than that. You have to *know*, honey." She leaned over and whispered in his ear. "These people got nothing on you. Believe me. Just look at them." She gestured with her chin. "They belong in a circus. I'm telling you," she said, "you got it made."

The rattle of a chain came from behind the double doors ahead. Only those toward the front of the line could've heard it, but the news traveled quickly, and in moments even those at the end of the line began pushing forward. Mrs. Shapiro took her son's hand in her own and squeezed it.

"Ready or not, here we go," she said. "Remember to smile now, remember to stand up straight."

The double doors swung open and a man stepped out onto the sidewalk. He started down the line, handing out entry forms as he went and shouting directions on how to fill them out. Mrs. Shapiro did exactly as she was told and gave the form to another man, smiling as she did so, when they passed through the doors.

On the stage inside a four-piece band was setting up their instruments. At the foot of it, on a raised platform, stood a table where the judges sat. When the seats in the auditorium were full, one of the judges hopped up on stage. He had a bulbous nose and long black sideburns and he wore a white tuxedo with a pink carnation in the pocket on his lapel. Mrs. Shapiro was certain she'd seen him before, but where she couldn't remember. He waved his hands over his head and the crowd grew quiet.

"What are we here for?" he shouted.

The auditorium was dead silent.

"C'mon now," he said. "We all know. A slot on *The Ed Sullivan Show*."

The crowd cheered. They clapped.

Mrs. Shapiro, who had chosen seats near the front row, reached over and squeezed Linus's knee. "That's for you, honey," she whispered. "These other people can just save everybody a lot of time and go home now." She laughed, expecting him to laugh with her, but he only yawned, less from lack of sleep than nervousness. His palms were sweaty and every now and then he felt himself short of breath.

The judge shouted again.

"Come to the table when I call your name. You have four minutes. *Four minutes*. Time's precious. Be careful how you use it."

Another judge handed him up a clipboard and he glanced at it, then looked into the audience.

"Mr. Hodge. George Hodge. Come on up."

Hodge was the man with the poodles.

He arranged all the dogs but one in a straight line on the stage. Then he introduced them—Sparky, Crystal, Sally, Rocket and Larry—pointing as he did so, each one barking after its name was called. Then, tipping his derby back, he squatted on his haunches and made a circle of his arms.

"Jump, Rocket. Jump through the hoop."

But the dog only sat there with its tongue hanging from its mouth. Hodge begged, he pleaded, and still the animal refused to budge. Suddenly Mr. Hodge leaped behind the dog and grinned at the audience. "You see that folks? Fast as lightning. Her name is apt." The audience groaned, while Mr. Hodge bobbed his head and laughed. He was about to launch into another routine, when the judge in the tuxedo stood up and clapped.

"Thank you, Mr. Hodge," he said. "Let's hear it for the poodle man."

Some applauded, most booed.

Mr. Hodge leashed his dogs and yanked them offstage.

"Next," the judge shouted. "The Dynamic Swensen Sisters."

They were twin redheads. One sang a medley of Paraguayan folk songs while strumming on a harp. The other snapped finger cymbals and swayed and rolled her hips.

Soon the judge rose from his chair again.

"Next."

A couple of actors did a scene from a Beckett play.

"Next."

A comedian.

"Next."

And on it went until the judge finally called on Eddie. Mrs. Shapiro nudged him and he rose shakily to his feet. "Let me look at you," she said, as she straightened the cap on his head. He forced a smile for her. "Don't be nervous now. Just do it like you do at home, just relax." She patted him on the rump. "Knock 'em dead, honey." He swallowed dryly once, then headed up the aisle to the table. With his hands clasped behind his back, and feeling queasy and light-headed, he stood before the judge in the tuxedo. "Your act, Eddie?"

Eddie cleared his throat but said nothing.

"Your act? You dance, you got a scene, or do you just stand there and look cute? We have a lot of people waiting on you." Again Linus swallowed, again he tried to speak but nothing came out. The judge rolled his eyes. "Nervous?" he said. Linus nodded. "Let me tell you something, Eddie." His voice suddenly grew soft. "We're all nervous, Eddie. We're nervous all the time in this goddamn town and that's what makes it work." He leaned to one side and looked behind him into the audience. "That your mother there? In the red?" Linus nodded again. "Go on, show us your stuff. Make her happy and then you can get out of here. Now," he said, "whatta you do?"

"I dance," he mumbled.

"Dance then."

"I sing, too."

"Sing and dance. What's the song?"

"'The Good Ship Lollypop.'" He looked down at his feet. "With my own words."

"You write 'em yourself?"

"Me and my mom."

"Do it, Eddie."

On stage the spotlight shone in his eyes. The auditorium looked dark and long, like a huge opened mouth. He could only hear them, the audience, the shifting of bodies in seats, the rustle of paper and the murmur of broken conversations. His heart pounded, as if it were pressing up against his lungs, sucking his breath away, and he felt weak in the knees.

The band struck the opening chords. But Linus didn't move. A few seconds passed and the music stopped. The judge shouted: "Do it, Eddie." The music began again and this time it took him.

> To the tip of the tippity top
> to the tip of the very very top
> I'm going to go far, I'm going
> to be a big big star....

Dancing, he was, tap tapping across the stage, toe to heel snapping clickety click, his voice rising powerfully from his chest like someone or something was working his mouth, pulling the words from his memory and moving his feet like they had never moved before. As his act came to an end, and the band ceased playing, Mrs. Shapiro rushed to the judge's table. The one in the tuxedo smiled up at her.

"That's my boy," she said. "What'd you think?"

"He's good."

Suddenly it came to her.

"I know you." She snapped her fingers. "You're Don Lane."

"That's right."

"I'll be," she said, shaking her head. "Don Lane. I never thought, well, I don't know why, I mean I love your show."

Don Lane looked at his wrist watch.

"I'd be glad to tell you more about it," he said, "if you wouldn't mind waiting. I should be done here by three."

She gave him her best smile. "I'd like that," she said.

Eddie approached them then, and his mother took him by the arm and led him up the aisle.

"Honey," she whispered. "Know who that was? Don Lane. *The* Don Lane. He's a big man, baby." She squeezed his arm. "And he wants to talk with us."

Mr. Lane drove a new red Cadillac with white leather upholstery, whitewall tires with spoked rims, and shark fins in the rear. Eddie sat in the back seat, waiting for them to come out of the bar down the block. They'd told him they were only going in for ten or fifteen minutes, but that was over an hour ago. The Shirley

Temple his mother had brought out to him had left his mouth feeling sticky and tasting sour. The plastic cup rested empty on the floorboard, and he crushed it under his shoe and then crossed his arms over his chest. Ahead he stared at the neon sign outside the bar. It was shaped like a martini glass with a big green onion in it that looked like it was rolling back and forth as the lights blinked on and off.

Finally the door swung open and they stepped out onto the sidewalk. His mother stopped for a moment and looked up at the sun and shielded her eyes. Her other hand held fast to Don Lane's arm. He was searching through her purse, his head bowed, and they were laughing. When he faced her, he leaned back and slipped a pair of sunglasses over her eyes. Eddie folded his hands into his lap and watched them approach, still laughing, swaying some as they walked. Mrs. Shapiro scooted into the front seat and glanced back at him. A silly smile spread across her face.

"Don't look so glum," she said. "We weren't gone *that* long." She reached out to pat his leg but he pulled away.

"You're such a spoilsport sometimes," she said. Mr. Lane slipped behind the wheel and put the transmission into gear. They drove.

"I was just telling your mother what a good little performer you are," Mr. Lane said. He rested his arm along the top of the seat and looked over his shoulder. "You're a champ." Eddie smiled politely. "I've seen a lot of talent. Believe me, I know what it is and you got it." In the rearview mirror Eddie watched the man's eyes; they were bloodshot, they were glazed.

"I've seen hundreds come and go and I tell you the god's honest truth not a dozen have half the stuff you got. You're a natural, Eddie." The back of Mr. Lane's neck was tanned, there were deep lines in the skin, and he smelled of cologne. He turned around in his seat again. "But let me give you some advice," he said. "Don't ever let success go to your head. You can be on top one day and the bottom the next."

Mrs. Shapiro chimed in.

"You listen to him now. Mr. Lane knows what he's talking about."

But he wasn't listening, he didn't want to listen. He pressed the window button and the glass slid down. Wind blew across his face. He watched the people on the sidewalk gawk at them in the big red Cadillac and he wondered, as they rolled slowly down the street, how much more he could endure, how much longer it would be before he was home.

"Why don't you sit up front, baby?"

"Huh?"

"Sit up front," his mother said.

Mr. Lane patted the seat between them.

"There's plenty of room," he said.

Reluctantly Eddie climbed over the back of the seat and settled between them. His mother smiled.

"How about a movie?" she said. "What movie do you want to see?"

Eddie shrugged.

"Take your pick," Mr. Lane said.

They were driving down Broadway through the theatre district. The marquee at the Orpheum advertised a Doris Day film, further up the block *Night of the Iguana* played at the Los Angeles, and the State was showing *Doctor X*. Mr. Lane drove slower. A long line of people stretched down the sidewalk from the box office of the Broadway. *Mary Poppins* was playing.

"Look at the crowd," Mrs. Shapiro said. She took her son's hand in her own and pressed it. "How about it? It's got to be good with all those people waiting to get in."

Don Lane maneuvered the Cadillac into the white zone in front of the box office. Mrs. Shapiro opened her door and got out.

"Give me a call when it's over and we'll pick you up," she said. "Don't leave the lobby. Don't stray. That clear?"

Eddie nodded.

She dug through her purse and handed him five dollars.

"Get yourself some popcorn."

Don Lane leaned over the seat and smiled.

"Aren't you forgetting something?"

In his hand was the sailor's cap, and he waved it at Eddie. Mrs. Shapiro took it from him and arranged it neatly on her son's head and gave him a peck on the cheek.

"Have fun now," she said.

Then she climbed back into the car and they drove off.

Eddie looked into the crowd and saw that some of them were staring at him. It was the suit, the ridiculous sailor's suit. He yanked off his cap and bowed his head and walked down the line, past the end of it, up the block.

At the State he bought a ticket and went inside. He passed through the lobby that smelled of popcorn and entered into the darkness of the auditorium and he chose a seat in an empty row. The movie had just begun. Blood dripped from the title letters on the big screen:

Doctor X

Eerie chamber music played over the credits.

    Connie Allen
    Henry Martin
    Myron McFall

He sunk back into his seat and watched. A close up of a scalpel. The blade glittered under the bright light over an operating table, where a beautiful woman lay unconscious. Slowly the camera pulled back, first revealing only the hand, then the arm, and finally the face of Doctor X. The music grew louder, deeper, the pounding of a drum like the beat of a heart. Henry Martin passed the tip of the scalpel under the woman's neck, as if he were tracing the line of her cheekbone. Eddie covered his eyes. Somewhere, in the back rows, a baby wailed.

He tried phoning his mother three times before he broke his word and left the theatre. On Broadway he spotted a bus pull to the curb and he made a dash for it. The doors hissed open but Eddie hesitated, as he wasn't sure where the bus was going, or if he was doing the right thing at all. But it was dark out now, he was worried, and he wasn't sure if they'd let him back into the theatre, even if that's what he wanted to do, and again he wasn't sure. The driver saw that he was scared.
  "You lost, sailor?"
  "I don't know."
  "Where do you live?" he said. "Maybe I can help."
  "The Royal Hotel."

The driver waved him on in.

"The old Royal it is," he said. "Step up and spill your pockets. For you it's front door service."

When the bus jerked forward, and he'd taken his seat across from an elderly woman, it struck him that something bad might've happened to his mother, and he began to worry even more. She'd never been late meeting him before and there had been lots of opportunities, considering all his dancing and acting lessons and how often she dropped him off and picked him up. But soon the bus rounded a corner came off Broadway and the neon sign over the Royal Hotel came into view. A sense of relief filled him, and he rose quickly to his feet and hurried for the back doors. As the bus came to a stop, he scanned the street for the red Cadillac but it was nowhere in sight.

Lily Hill was working the desk when he dashed by her.

"Don't run in the lobby," she hollered. "That's the last time I'll say it. You're going to hurt somebody."

He ignored her, pressed the elevator button and stepped back to wait. On the panel above the door the number six was lit up. He rang the bell again but the light didn't move, and he gave up and raced past Lily to the stairwell.

"What'd I just tell you?" she shouted.

Up the stairs, two at a pop, he ran. By the time he made it to the fourth floor he was panting and had broken a sweat. He reached for the door knob, found it unlocked and went inside.

A half-empty bottle of gin rested on the kitchen table. Beside it were an opened telephone book, some papers, two glasses and a wrinkled quarter of lime.

"Mom?"

No answer.

"Mom?"

Her voice was groggy.

"Just a second," she said.

He heard the squeak of box springs, then her footsteps on the carpet, then the clink of hangers in her closet. A moment later the door to the bedroom opened and she came out dressed in her bathrobe. In her hand was a hairbrush.

"I was about to call a taxi."

"I took the bus."

"I'm sorry," she said. "Really." She started for the kitchen table, a bit unsteadily. "So long as you made it home. That's what matters." Her hair was rumpled and she pulled the brush through it, caught on a tangle and winced.

"C'mere," she said.

He went to her, but he went slowly, with a certain cautiousness. She put her arms around him and hugged him. Through her robe he felt the heat, the warmth of her soft breasts and the pounding of her heart.

"You didn't make *The Ed Sullivan Show*," she said. "But look here."

She reached for the papers on the table and turned to the last page. She put her finger on the last line and smiled.

"Find a pen, baby," she said. "You just got yourself a real Beverly Hills agent."

*

11

He found himself in the hospital three days later watching *Animal Crackers*. The television was suspended from a steel bar above the door. Only a few minutes before he and the man in the next bed had been laughing at the great Groucho, but now that man was on his way into surgery and the jokes sounded flat. Henry reached for the remote control in his lap and pressed one of the buttons. The screen flickered, then another picture appeared—a soap opera. He pressed the off-button and for a while he stared at the gray tube, listening to it crackle inside the cabinet as it cooled. Outside, down the hall, he heard the swish and slop of a wet mop on the floor.

There was another set of controls on the bed railing, and he ran his hand along them and pressed another button. The top half of the mattress rose until he was sitting far enough forward to reach the phone. He dialed his home number and let it ring and ring, hoping Eddie would answer. The kid had yet to visit him or even call and the old man was worried. Yesterday morning his bedside phone had rung and he'd hoped it was Eddie, but instead he was greeted by the overly cheerful voice of a salesman from Sentinel Hospital Supplies who wanted to sell him a motorized wheelchair. Medicare, the man said, would pay for it. The model Henry ordered would arrive late tomorrow afternoon.

Six rings, seven, then eight.

Henry sighed and returned the receiver to its cradle.

The small of his back, his hips and his good leg, ached with stiffness. Too many hours, too many days in bed. He leaned over the railing, stretching his spine, his muscles. On the floor rested a bed pan, its white inside marked with fine black lines from scrubbing it with cleansers. The nurses had insisted he use it and he had, begrudgingly, always with some embarrassment, always with some shame. But they promised him he'd be able to use the bathroom himself soon, if he was careful.

A young nurse, for they all seemed young to Henry, entered the room. She was pushing a wheelchair.

"How you feeling this morning, Mr. Martin?"

"Fine," he said. "Fine enough to get out of here anyway."

She helped him from the bed into the wheelchair and led him out of the room, down a hall and into another room where a doctor waited. The nurse slipped a blood pressure wrap around his good arm and pumped it up. Henry watched the mercury rise in the gauge mounted on the wall. A vein throbbed on the inside of his arm and pulsed in rhythm with his heartbeat. The doctor lifted Henry's gown above his knee, took a pen from his pocket and, with the blunt end of it, began to poke at the old man's leg.

"Can you feel that?" he said.

"No."

"What about here?"

"Nothing."

"Now?"

Henry shook his head.

"Not a damn thing, doc."

The mercury fell in jerks.

"One-eighty over seventy," the nurse said.

She removed the wrap from his arm and set it in its tray beside the gauge.

"Too high," the doctor said. "Way too high. You have to learn to relax."

He took his clipboard from the top of the sink and scribbled a note, then slipped the pen behind his ear.

"I need to run a couple of more tests," he said. "You'll be here at least another day."

"Doc?"

"Yes?"

Henry nodded at his leg.

"What do you think? Will I be able to walk on it again?"

"I can't say, Mr. Martin."

"An outside guess?"

"Just try not to worry about it for now," he said. "You had a stroke, a bad one but I've seen worse, and you need rest. Nurse Davies will give you something to help you sleep."

At that the doctor left and the nurse wheeled Henry back to his room and gave him two red capsules and a cup of water to wash them down. When she had gone he sat up and reached for the phone on the nightstand and made another call.

"Department of Transportation."

"Is Mr. Waters in?"

"May I ask who's calling?"

"Henry Martin."

"I'm sorry, but he's in a meeting right now. Can I take a message?"

"Tell him I'm ready to talk turkey."

"Talk what?"

"Turkey," he said. "Business. I'm ready to make a deal."

"Hang on."

A dozen seconds passed.

"Hello?"

"Mr. Waters?"

"Speaking."

"I have a proposition."

"Let's hear it."

Henry cleared his throat.

"I'll sell if you'll drop the charges."

"Good to hear it, Mr. Martin. One thing we both don't need is bad publicity. I'll have my secretary draw up the papers and get them off to you first thing tomorrow morning."

"Fine," Henry said. "Have her send them to twelve-zero-two Wilshire Boulevard. Room twenty-three." He returned the receiver to its cradle.

Soon the red capsules took effect and when he woke up it was morning. Sunlight leaked through a bent slat in the Venetian blinds over the window and fell across his face. The air was warm and thick with the odor of antiseptic and he was sweating. For a moment, blinking against the bar of light, he didn't remember where he was and he couldn't catch his breath. Somewhere in the room a man groaned, and from somewhere down the hall he heard the faint sound of a radio. He pulled the sheet back and looked down at his leg. The hair on his calf had worn away over the years, the skin against cloth, friction and time. He ran his hand down his thigh and willed the leg to move but it did nothing. He tried to wiggle his toes but again, nothing. One moment he'd been sitting on the toilet in the bathroom at Clifton's and in the next there was a slight popping noise inside of his head, then a tingling down his spine and the leg was numb.

Again he heard the man groan and he wondered if he was struggling in pain or if it was the drugs or only a nightmare. He thought of Eddie, he thought of the play. He pictured himself in a wheelchair and he lay back in bed and turned his face into his pillow. How could he get up the stairs to his house? Or to the theatre? How could he make his own bed or take a shower without help? And his hand, even when the cast came off, could he trust it? Not since Henry was seventeen years old and had left home had he ever let someone handle his chores for him, let alone help him to the damn bathroom.

When he looked up he saw Evelyn standing in the doorway, smiling. She had on a blue denim skirt and her gray hair was pulled back in a ponytail. Tucked under her arm, folded into a tube, were a couple of magazines. She went to the bed and sat down beside him.

"How's the leg?"

He shrugged.

She took the sheet between her fingers and made like she was going to pull it back, expose him. Henry grinned and held the sheet down with his good arm.

"Since when have you been so modest?"

"You come all the way here just to give an old friend a hard time?" he said. "Aren't you supposed to be on the set?"

"It's Sunday, Henry. I can think of a lot of better things to do."

She'd brought him copies of *Time* and *Newsweek* and now she put them on the nightstand on a pile of other magazines that she'd given him. It was her third visit in as many days.

"Any word from Eddie?"

"Hasn't he come by yet?"

Henry shook his head.

"I think he blames himself," she said.

"Why?" he said. "For what?"

"The night it happened, when he was driving me back to get my car, he kept saying it was his fault," she said. "He kept saying that he put too much pressure on you."

"That's bullshit, it had nothing to do with him."

He sat forward and she helped him slip a pillow behind his back.

"I wonder if you could do me a favor," he said, slowly, as if he wasn't really sure that he had the right to ask. "I won't be going back to my house. I'm bailing out."

"Where?" she said.

"The Wilshire Home."

"Oh shit."

"I don't want to hear it," he said. "I've made all the arrangements. Somebody went by yesterday to pick up a few of my things."

There was a silence.

"I've tried calling Eddie I don't know how many times. But I can't get an answer. If he's there, he sure as hell ain't answering," he said. "I'd appreciate if you'd swing by when you have a chance and leave him a note. Tell him he has to get his stuff out. Tell him if he wants any of the furniture to go ahead and take it, and what he can't use give it to the Salvation Army."

"Henry," she said. "I really think you ought to reconsider."

"I already told you, it's not open for debate," he said.

The other patient in the room, the one who'd been

groaning, began to snore. There was a privacy curtain for each of the different beds and Evelyn reached up and pulled the one around them closed.

"You don't want to live in some lousy rest home," she said. She leaned over and kissed Henry, first on the neck, then his lips. "When's the nurse come in?" she whispered. He said he didn't know. She grinned. She unbuttoned her blouse and slipped quickly out of her skirt.

"The worst they can do," she said, "is kick me out."

It had been ten or twelve years since he'd made love, and at the sight of her body he felt the breath go out of him. Evelyn was a beautiful woman still. She pulled back the sheet, lifted his hospital gown and gently kissed him on the stomach. Her lips felt warm.

"I'm on medication," he said.

"So?"

"High blood pressure pills, too."

"Who isn't at our age?" she said. "Relax. I'll get you in the mood."

She climbed on top of him and began to rock, slowly, back and forth.

"You're too ornery for a rest home," she said. "It's no place for you."

He ran his hands over her breasts, then down her sides to her hips and held her there while she moved against him.

"You'll regret it, I know you will."

"There," he said.

"Good as new."

He was inside her now. She rocked faster. Henry raised his head and smiled, for his leg, bouncing on the mattress in time to their beat, looked as if it had suddenly come back to life.

12

Linus went on a drunk. A great drunk. A magnificent drunk, a wallowing, self-pitying drunk that began the night Henry entered the hospital. Now he was lost in a haze, somewhere between sleep and consciousness, curled up in the backseat of his Olds 88 parked on Hill Street in downtown Los Angeles between a taco stand and an all-night porno shop. The morning sweeper, its round brush slapping against the curb, its motor whirring, passed slowly on the street. The Olds shook. Linus grumbled. Wind? Vibrations from the sweeper? But the car continued to shake, more powerfully, and then came the ring of metal on asphalt. He bolted upright and spotted a little kid, not more than seven or eight years old, running across the street with a crowbar in one hand and a pillow case in the other. On the sidewalk he'd left one, a hubcap. Linus cursed under his breath. The little punk. Shouldn't he have been in school?

His temples throbbed, his mouth was dry. He got out of the car, picked up the hubcap, threw it in the backseat and headed down the block to the Eightball. There it was still a dollar a shot, and he took a seat at the bar and ordered himself a round. Beside him sat a man who'd lost his eye in Vietnam, a fact which Linus knew only because he'd been drinking with him the night before, but at a different bar somewhere up the street. Linus kept his head lowered and drank in silence. It was too early yet to talk. After a couple of more shots he held his hand over his glass to see if it was steady, and it was—the rock.

He nodded to himself.

First he had to get new pictures, some good headshots that would do him justice—not like the others, the old ones when he was still practically a teenager. The poses had been stiff, the smiles forced. He needed a photographer who could make him relax, keep him moving and then freeze him at just the right moment for that certain special look. But the good ones cost. He needed decent clothes too. He needed a PO box. He needed a new pair of shoes. And some sun. Some color in those cheeks.

If anyone wondered where he'd been all these years, and why he hadn't worked, he could tell them he'd been out of town. In New York, say, or the midwest, doing little theatre. Shakespeare. Chekhov. O'Neill. Lie, he thought, just lie. Nobody's going to check on you. Linus ordered a beer to settle the whiskey, then dug into his pocket for some change and went to the phone at the back of the bar. He dropped a coin into the slot, took a deep breath and dialed.

"Broom Artists Agency."

"Is Annie in?"

"Who's calling?"

"Eddie Shapiro."

The mouthpiece smelled of tobacco and he held it away from his face as he waited. In his mind he saw Annie as she looked seven years before. Tall. Like his mother. She liked silver and turquoise bracelets and usually wore her hair short. He drew his finger down the side of the phone.

"Hello?"

"Yes?"

"She's in a meeting right now. Is there something I can help you with?"

"I doubt it."

"If it regards representation, we're not taking on any new clients."

"I'm not a new client."

"I'm sorry," she said. "What's your name again?"

But there was no point.

"Forget it," he said. "I'll call back later."

Quietly, after a moment, he put the receiver on its hook and wandered out of the bar.

At the liquor store on the corner he bought a pint of cheap bourbon and drove out to the Royal Hotel. The demo crew was nowhere in sight; it must've been Saturday or Sunday, he'd lost count of the days. He climbed out of the car and went up the marble steps. In place of the doors were sheets of plywood, and he kicked and pulled at one until it fell into the lobby with a swoosh of air, a cloud of dust. Look, he thought. Just look what they've done. Bare wires dangled from a hole in the ceiling where a wonderful crystal chandelier had once hung. The long front counter carved out of walnut had been pried up and hauled away. All that remained were the bolts in the floor. Linus pulled the pint of bourbon from his back pocket, cracked the seal, drank and shuddered. The wrought iron gate over the elevator had been ripped off its track. Capping the bottle, he headed up the stairs.

Now and then he had to stop and rest. Once, between the second and third floors, he missed a step and stumbled. He grabbed for the railing, except it wasn't there. Some punk, some worker maybe, had stolen it or had torn it off for fun. He looked over the edge. It was a long drop to the lobby.

On the sixth floor he leaned against the wall and glanced down the hall where he and his mother had once lived. The door to their room was open and inside, on the floor next to a dirty mattress, lay an empty bottle of *Thunderbird*. A pair of orange pants rested neatly folded on the windowsill, and the rancid odor of urine hung in the air.

"Hey," he shouted. "Anybody here?"

His voice echoed.

He continued up the stairs until there were no more to climb and he had reached the Gold Room. Where the tall double doors used to be, inlaid with panes of frosted glass and etched with cherubs and grape vines, now only hinges remained. The mirror behind the bar was shattered and the bar itself, the cabinets and shelves, all the chairs and tables were gone. Only the long row of stool poles missing the seats remained bolted to the floor. Linus shook his head. Across the wall somebody had spraypainted *Heavy Metal* in blood red. On the floor beside his foot he spotted a lewd picture of a woman torn from a hardcore magazine. He took another drink, and as he raised his head he noticed the high, rounded ceiling, the mural—untouched. He stared and stared. The nude men and women were smiling at him, leering actually, and then suddenly he thought he heard laughter. The figures began to move. Dozens of silver fish that surrounded them shifted in the sunlight beneath the surface of a pond. Linus squinted, his eyes watered and stung. He rubbed them and looked again. The fish leaped at him in a stream of bright silver and he turned away. In the shattered mirror he saw the face of an ancient man with skin coarse like a lizard's, teeth yellowed and cracked, his hair sparse and oily and the eyes glazed. The fish were slipping down the back of Linus's shirt, one after another, cold and slick.

He threw the bottle across the room. It busted against the pillar in a shower of glass. And then he ran, slapping and beating at the fish wildly, with both hands, while screaming as if for his life.

Back at the Olds he got a grip on himself and drove to the house. There he found an envelope with his name on it tacked to the front door. He opened it carefully and read the note inside, then once again more slowly. It was signed by Evelyn. Linus tossed it on the kitchen table and went to Henry's bedroom. The bed was stripped to the mattress and the pictures and the masks on the wall were gone. The dresser drawers had been emptied and the closet was bare except for a few hangers. He stretched out on the mattress, intending only to rest for a few minutes, to clear his head so that he could think about what to do next, but a moment later he fell asleep.

When he finally woke the walls were trembling. Pots clattered in the kitchen, and the floor beneath him groaned and creaked as if the hardwood were being pulled apart at the joints. He jumped out of bed and stumbled down the hall to the living room and yanked the drapes open.

In the distance a cloud of gray dust rose into the sky. As it dissipated he saw the wrecking ball more clearly, dangling from its cable through the neck of the crane. It brought the ball up and back and positioned it for the next blow. He took in a deep breath. The ball, released, glided silently through the air into the top story of the Royal Hotel. Concrete, glass and plaster crashed to the earth. Again the ground shook; the iron ball swung gently back and forth in the sky.

The Royal Hotel sign clung to the edge of the roof and, turning, barely hanging on, suddenly fell free.

In the kitchen, the phone rang. Linus let the drapes close and went to answer it.

The voice was a woman's.

"Is this the Second Story Theatre?"

"Yeah."

"Are there still seats for the Wednesday opening?"

He pulled the receiver from his ear and looked at the note on the kitchen table. A heaviness filled his chest. The Wilshire Home, he thought. A fucking tomb. He closed his eyes a moment, then opened them slowly. Once more the iron ball hit, once more the vibrations moved through the streets and shook the house deep to its foundation. His head throbbed. He needed another drink, a double shot, except this time he figured he'd wait on it.

He returned the receiver to his ear.

"What day is it?" he said.

"Huh?"

"The day," he said. "What *day* is it?"

"Monday."

"Good," he said. "That's all I needed to know. How many tickets do you want?"

13

The Wilshire Home was near MacArthur Park, on the same street that housed a video arcade and a Salvadoran restaurant, an old Spanish theatre and two liquor stores with bars over the windows. The sign hung from an iron fire escape above the front door. Secure Building, it read. Color TV. Qualified Nurse on Staff 24 Hours. He had his room outside a poorly lit hall toward the back of the building, across from the kitchen. Exhaust fans on the roof went on and off every hour or so and the noise had kept him awake most of the night. The bed was a single, he'd had a double at home and he thought that that might've also had something to do with his sleeplessness. But he'd get used to it, he told himself. It was only a matter of time. From his wheelchair, he ran his hand along the mattress and wondered how many others had slept and died here.

His clothes hung in an open closet with a floral print drape for its door. Evelyn had been kind enough to drive him over the night before. She'd stayed a while to group his shirts with his shirts, his pants with his pants, and arrange his shoes on the closet floor. An orderly had hung his pictures and masks for him. Henry wheeled himself over to the sliding glass door that looked out on the concrete courtyard. In a lawn chair, beneath a patio umbrella spotted with mildew, he noticed an old woman in a white gown. She stared down at her slippers and her lips moved as if she were talking to herself. Nearby stood a ping-pong table that had been left to the sun and rain too many seasons; the top sagged and dipped in the middle and the net was missing. It was sunny, and he thought of going outside, but he decided against it. He reached for the chrome hoops around the wheels and winced as he pushed himself away from the window. The muscles in his arms and chest were sore but they'd toughen up, he thought. They'd toughen up soon enough.

In the bathroom a naked bulb burned from the ceiling. Stainless steel bars were mounted on both sides of the toilet, the tank top was cracked, and a leaking valve made a hissing noise from inside of it. He'd already complained about the valve. And he'd complained about the fungus growing on the shower tiles, too, after Evelyn had pointed it out to him. So far nothing had been done, but then it had only been a day and he couldn't see any reason to get riled yet. Evelyn had left the room mad. Or was it in disgust? He couldn't tell but she'd grabbed her purse and all but ran. She had offered him her home "until he could make a better decision" and he'd declined.

Through the wall he heard a radio playing *mariachi* music. In another room someone coughed. He looked at the telephone on the nightstand and thought of calling Evelyn and apologizing, but for what he wasn't sure. He thought of turning on the TV but there wasn't anything he wanted to watch. The clock on his dresser showed a-quarter-to-twelve and he wondered if he ought to wander over to the dining hall for lunch. Yesterday he'd seen a man refuse to eat and then try to leave the table. He fell out of his chair and he couldn't get back up and the aide who served the meals let him stay there until he apologized. He had given her a hard time. That much Henry admitted. There was a knock on the door.

"Yeah?"

"It's me."

He wheeled himself to the door, unlocked it and let him in.

"I'm sorry," Linus said.

"There's nothing to be sorry about."

"I should've visited."

Henry shrugged.

"It's no big deal."

"You're not mad?"

"What for?"

"I just thought, you know."

"Come in," he said. "Have a seat."

But instead Linus went to the sliding glass door and looked out on the stark concrete courtyard. The old woman was still sitting in the lawn chair, staring at her slippers and talking to herself.

"They have a recreation room here," Henry said. "Pool tables. Snooker. Checkers. Chess. You name it." Linus had his back to him and he couldn't judge the expression on his face. "The Rainbow Girls are coming to sing tomorrow, too, and I understand they're pretty damn good." A pause. "It's not as bad as you think."

Linus turned around.

"Cut the shit," he said. "This place is fucking depressing."

Henry said nothing.

"C'mon, man," Linus said. "Let's get out of here. Let's go for a walk."

He moved behind the chair to push but Henry batted his hand away.

"Just get the door," he said.

They headed down the hall.

"Smells like piss in here," Linus said.

"It does not."

"You can't smell that," he said, "then you can't smell nothing."

"Hey," Henry said, "if you don't have anything nice to say keep your mouth shut."

In the lobby two old men sat on a tattered sofa. One dressed in a flannel bathrobe was asleep, while the other read from a copy of *Reader's Digest*. Linus stepped by them and tried to open the door but it was locked.

A woman at the front desk called to them.

"Mr. Martin?"

"What?"

"Where you going?"

"For a walk."

"You have to sign out first," she said, "and you have to sign in when you come back."

She passed him a ledger and he scrawled his name, knowing, as he did so, that Linus took some kind of perverse pleasure from it.

He whispered in Henry's ear.

"Just like a kid again. Like the Cub Scouts, eh? Like school."

"Hush now."

Outside on the street Linus told him that he wanted to go to the park.

"We'll check out the lake," he said.

"It's polluted," Henry said. "The pigeons are diseased and the place is overrun with drug dealers."

"Always looking on the bright side, eh?" he said. "Surprise me for a change."

MacArthur Park was a few blocks away and rather than walk Linus suggested that they drive. His Olds was parked at the curb and he unlocked the door and nodded to Henry.

"Can you get in all right?"

He gave him a dirty look, then wheeled himself to the door, took hold of the frame and lifted himself to his good leg, pivoted, ducked his head, and dropped into the front seat.

"It folds up," he said, "the chair."

Linus stowed it in the trunk, then hopped into the car and soon they were cruising by the park. At the Sixth and Alvarado entrance a group of Mexican men stood around smoking and talking and further down, on a green sloping hill, a family was having a party. In the tree above them hung a Donald Duck *piñata* and a little girl swung at it furiously with a baseball bat. She wore a blindfold made out of a red bandanna. *Salsa* blasted from a big tape player resting on the bench.

"Slow down," Henry said. "There's a spot ahead."

"Where?"

He pointed.

"Right there."

"Where?"

"Behind that truck."

But Linus drove past it.

"Maybe I can't smell worth a damn," he said, "but you're blind as hell."

Linus looked at him and smiled.

"Good to see you again, man. Good to hear you bitch."

He stepped down on the gas and swerved around a car ahead.

Henry gripped the dashboard.

"It's opening night," Linus said. "You're out of your mind if you think I'm taking you back to that fucking morgue."

Scene three, take four.

She'd blown it every time. Evelyn tossed her head back. Her lips moved slightly as she silently repeated her lines over and over. Beside her she heard the cameraman, the soft electric hiss of his dolly rolling forward then backward, gauging distance.

The director shouted.

"Ready."

Evelyn nodded.

A buzzer sounded and she stiffened. The spotlights shining on her seemed to blur, separate, double, then separate.

"*Action.*"

Stagehands froze in place.

Again the spotlights separated, converged, separated. The camera boy held the clapboard in front of the lens. Evelyn heard the slap of wood on wood, then his voice.

"Scene three, take four."

Danny swung open the false door on the set and entered center stage. There was a nervous, apprehensive look in his eyes.

>   MACON
> What'd the police say?
>
>   TILL
> That they found our witness this
> morning.
>
>   MACON
> Is she willing to testify?
>
>   TILL
> Not anymore. She's dead.
> It looks like....

Her mind went blank. The director sliced his hands through the air like an umpire calling the out.

"Cut," he shouted.

She bowed her head.

"It looks like what?" he said. "Huh? Like *we're going to have to find her daughter to testify, Macon.*" He had on a baseball cap turned around backwards and he yanked it off. "Take a break. Let's all take a break. Ten minutes."

Rarely, she thought, as she shuffled off the set, had she messed up a take twice, let alone five times. But she hadn't looked at the script until this morning at breakfast. Like the job or not she had a responsibility to do it well or not at all and her performance had shamed her. She went to the coffee stand and poured herself a cup. In her pocket she always carried a tin of aspirin, and she took it out and shook a couple into her hand. Danny approached as she swallowed them with the coffee.

He made a clucking noise with his tongue.

"I saw the ad in the paper for that little play you're doing."

"It's been cancelled."

"Lucky for you," he said. "A play and a series, at your age it's not wise to push yourself." He leaned closer to her. "You look pale. You might want to try a darker blush."

"Get out of my face."

"Then memorize your lines."

"That's all it really means to you, doesn't it?" she said. "Memorization. You've never done good work in your life, Danny, and when this show dies so does your career."

At that she turned on her heels and headed to the padded entry chamber, opened the door, then the other that led outside. The camera boy caught up with her a moment later.

"You got a call, Ms. Richardson. Some guy named Eddie. Said it was an emergency."

"I'll take it my dressing room."

The Olds was parked next to the phone booth outside a Chevron station on Melrose. Henry rolled down his window.

"Eddie?"

"What?"

"This isn't a good idea."

"Quit worrying."

"I'm in a wheelchair."

"Improvise, man, improvise. You're an actor."

Then he turned away and began to talk into the receiver.

What he said, Henry couldn't hear. He lit a cigarette, settled into his seat and watched the cars pass on the street.

Danny paced the set. He held his fingertips to his temples as if he was concentrating intensely on his character.

The director spoke softly.

"Ready?"

Danny nodded.

"Get Evelyn," the director said. He motioned to Larry, the A.D., who hurried off to her dressing room.

The boom man swung the mike around and lowered it over Danny's head, though he kept it out of the frame. The cameraman spun around on his stool so that he faced the eyepiece, and the gaffer shouted for his men on the catwalk to get ready. Another assistant held a light meter to Danny's chin and discovered a glare.

"Make-up," he called.

A girl rushed from off the set with a cosmetic pad and dabbed some rouge on Danny's chin.

"Get my left cheek, too, babe, while you're at it," he said. "It feels a little damp."

She obeyed, then backed away. Danny sniffed, paced again, rolled his shoulders and neck to loosen up. The set grew quiet. On the catwalk an electrician shifted his weight from one leg to the other and the steel grates creaked. The director looked up and glared at him.

A short while later the A.D. returned out of breath.

"She's gone."

"No," he said. "Don't say it."

"Her car, too."

The director made a fist.

"That's it," he said. "It's over. We're not babysitters. Call Mr. Rosen and tell him she walked on us again."

Danny spoke up.

"What'd I tell you?" he said. "She's a bitch."

"Stuff it," the director said. "The show's garbage without her."

Evelyn looked in the rearview mirror. Behind her the studio grew fainter, and when she turned the bend past Forest Lawn it was gone. She wondered if she'd made a mistake but the thought passed quickly. It wasn't as if she needed the money anymore, and in terms of glamour *Testimony* offered her only a false sense of it. In terms of art, though she'd known it from the start, it had little. At the top of the hill she depressed the clutch and downshifted. The muscles in her hips felt pleasantly sore from having made love to Henry.

She accelerated.

The broken white line appeared to blur so that for a moment it looked solid, as if it were reaching up to her, then it was rushing beneath the car and dividing again in the mirror. She thought of the script, the one ahead, and whether there was anything in it that she hadn't committed firmly to heart. But this one she knew well, inside and out, each phrase, each word, every line she planned to deliver, every move she planned to make.

From beginning to end.

There would be no lapses this time around. No silence. No mistakes.

14

Where the Royal Hotel had once stood now there was only sky and a fine view of the freeway under construction beyond it. As the dump trucks rolled down the street, their beds heavy with chunks of concrete and steel scrap, Linus and Henry and Evelyn had their dress rehearsal. All afternoon they coordinated their exits and entrances. They polished gestures, reactions and cues. Finally an hour before the opening, Henry wheeled himself backstage to the light panel and called out to Evelyn as he flipped the different switches.

"Red?"

"On."

"Blue?"

"On."

While they continued to check the spots Linus set up an old card table at the foot of the theatre stairs.

On top of it he placed a small metal cash box and a stack of programs. Then, on the front door, he tacked a copy of a poster that he'd made. He did the same with more of them, all around the front of the house, so that when he'd finished the place looked like one big bulletin board.

HENRY MARTIN
&
EVELYN RICHARDSON

Starring In
The Great...The Grand...The Original...

THE ROYAL HOTEL

In Honor Of The Demise of The
Historical Landmark

Henry Martin as Gary Lombardo
Evelyn Richardson as Lily Hill
Edward Shapiro as Bert Goodman

Provocative
Innovative
Powerful

One Performance Only

—TONIGHT—
at 8 P.M. SHARP

at

The One and Only Second Story Theatre

As he was tacking up the last poster a man in a Volvo stopped on the street. He leaned over to the passenger's side and waved a copy of the flyer at Linus.

"This the Second Story Theatre?"

"You got it."

"Evelyn Richardson is performing here?" he said, "*the* Richardson?"

"Who else?"

The man looked at the old place, frowned and then drove off. But a minute later a couple of other cars pulled to the curb and the people, there must've been ten or eleven of them, got out and headed to the doors. Down the street the headlights of another car approached. By a quarter to eight they had a full house.

Linus posted a *Sold Out* sign on the theatre door, hurried backstage and dressed into his bellhop's costume. Then he took his place at the light panel and checked his watch. At a minute to eight he signalled to Henry and Evelyn by holding up one finger. Silently he counted off the last three seconds, then he nodded to them and cut the lights. The theatre fell into darkness. He turned on the tape player and the cacophony of diesel engines, of falling wreckage and the growl of tractors flowed through the speakers. He let the spots rise slowly as he lowered the volume. Illuminated centerstage was a table with a phone on it, a cot and dresser to the side, and upstage was a wooden grill painted black to resemble the iron grates of an elevator door.

One beat. Two. Three.

Henry wheeled himself onto the stage, stopped beside the cot and drew his hand along the steel frame. When Evelyn entered the applause broke out. She waited until it was quiet before she launched into her opening line.

LILY: The last tenant packed up and left this morning. It's just you, me and Bert now.

Henry cleared his throat.

GARY: Cowards.

The play progressed quickly and without a hitch. Linus's role was small in the first act, he entered with brief announcements then left, but come the second it grew. When he heard his cue he took a sip of water, adjusted the collar of his costume and hurried out on stage. He carried a doctor's satchel with him.

At this point Gary Lombardo was near death. Linus opened the bag, removed a pint of whiskey, uncapped it and handed it to him. The old man took it and drank.

BERT: You feel better now, sir?

GARY: Is he still there?

He went to the window and opened it. As he looked out, the sound of the heavy machinery grew louder.

BERT: Yes, sir.

GARY: Don't let the man out of your sight.

He took another drink.

GARY: He's getting closer, he's getting bigger and fatter. Can you smell him?

BERT: Yes.

GARY: Shut the window, Bert. I can't stand it.

Linus closed the window, went to the doctor's bag and took out a tourniquet. He rolled up Henry's sleeve and fastened the strap around his arm. Henry looked up at him with tender eyes.

GARY: You've been good to me. You've taken fine care of Lily and the hotel.

BERT: You've been good to me, too, sir.

GARY: It's been a long time, hasn't it?

BERT: You're back now, that's all that matters.

GARY: But we have to stop him.

BERT: The old fighting spirit, eh? You'll be at the dance tonight. In the Gold Room. Everyone's expecting you.

GARY: Look at me, Bert. Bones. Nothing but bones. Who wants a sick man?

Linus removed a syringe from the bag and fired it into the old man's arm. He closed his eyes, and as the morphine took effect the sounds of the equipment and the falling wreckage gave way to the silence.

BERT: Better, sir?

GARY: Much, much, much better.

BERT: Then you'll come tonight? To the Gold Room?

GARY: Listen... the noise, it's stopped.

BERT: Just for a while. (beat) Don't disappoint your guests. Promise you'll be there. Dance tonight, sir. Dance and it'll come back.

Strauss's *Blue Danube* played softly in the background. He wheeled Henry to the middle of the stage. They danced.

The music rose.

They danced until the lights had faded.

They danced until it was dark and until all they could hear was the surrounding roar of cheers and applause.

15

There was champagne. There were cheese and crackers, a bottle of good cognac and music for those who remained after the play to mingle and drink and congratulate them. Several people wanted Evelyn's autograph and she obliged. Another, a young film buff who knew all of Henry's films, approached him with an old still from *Pearl of Blood* and asked him to sign it. He was flattered, he was impressed. A reporter from the *L.A. Times* was there too and he snapped their picture, asked them lots of questions and told them he planned to run an article in the Sunday *Calendar*. And someone from *Variety* said she intended to write a strong review.

When the last guest had left Henry asked Linus for a ride back to the Wilshire Home.

"Absolutely not," he said.

"Evelyn?"

"Nope."

"I've been thinking," Linus said.

"About what?"

"Renting an apartment together."

"Seriously?"

"Seriously," Evelyn said. "We've already discussed it."

"I don't know," Henry said.

"Listen," Linus said, "if it doesn't work out we can always split up. But let's not worry about it now. Just give it a shot. You don't want to go back to that hell hole."

"Ground floor apartment?"

"Whatever," he said. "I'll build you a ramp if you want."

Evelyn poured them another glass of champagne.

"Tonight," she said, "you can both stay with me and in the morning we'll look for a place. Okay? No more talk."

Linus went backstage and packed up the last of his things and carried them out to the Olds. Then he helped Henry down the stairs and into the front seat. Evelyn said she'd meet them at her house, gave Henry a kiss and left.

In the Olds, as they rode down the street, he turned to Linus and asked him to drive past what remained of the Royal Hotel.

"What for?"

"Old times' sake. I don't know," he said. "Do I have to have a reason?"

When they'd arrived he told him to park and get his wheelchair from the trunk.

"If I ever needed your help," he said, "I need it now. Understand? I can't give the bastards the satisfaction."

The streets were deserted and the crane rested idle in the moonlight. Henry wheeled himself to the ladder, grabbed hold of it and lifted himself out of the chair.

"Give me a boost."

Linus just stood there.

"You going to help or not?"

"I shouldn't," Linus said, as if to himself. "I really shouldn't."

But he gave him the boost and, with it, Henry was able to pull himself up into the driver's seat.

"Now run get me a crowbar," he said, "and a flashlight, too."

There was a steel coverplate over the instrument panel. When he returned with the crowbar, Henry slipped the tip of it under the plate, braced himself with his good arm, bore down with all his weight and snapped the cover off at the hinge. Beneath it was the starter button.

"Hop on," he said.

"You're crazy."

He laughed.

"You just realized that now?"

As soon as he'd climbed up beside him, Henry pulled out the choke and pressed the starter button. The engine growled, sputtered, then died. He stepped on the accelerator and tried it again and this time it fired. The cab vibrated. A burst of heat and smoke rose from the exhaust pipe, and Linus held on tight. There were three stick levers on the dash and a shift on the column. Henry pulled one on the dash. Another motor whirred. Through the windshield they watched the cable slip along the reels inside the crane until all the slack was taken up. With a jolt, the great iron wrecking ball rose from the earth.

"You'll have to help me steer this monster," he said.

"How?"

"Like a car. A big one." He paused. "Then again,

the way you drive maybe I'm better off doing it myself." He pulled another lever and the crane moved to the left. Another and it turned right. The ball swung from side to side. He shifted it into gear and the machine lurched forward.

"Hang on now," he said. "We're going for a little ride."

Down the middle of the street they advanced with the ball swinging and the engine rumbling and spewing exhaust. They passed the lot where the Royal Hotel had once stood. They passed the condemned stores and shops, some already reduced to rubble, others still intact.

They passed the boarded-up apartments on the next block and finally they came to the house. He ran the machine straight over the sidewalk and onto the front lawn. He pulled another lever, a motor hummed. The crane rose slowly until the great iron ball hung over the theatre.

Linus closed his eyes and imagined the earth quaking beneath them.

Silence.

Briefly Henry considered changing his mind, then he reached for the lever. He pulled.

The silence, just before impact, was like thunder.

THE RAT BOY

a short story

My mother caught Roy Lambert looking through her bedroom window at a quarte-to-four in the morning. She could have called the cops but instead she phoned Mrs. Lambert. Roy was twenty-one and living at home. This was 1970 and he had returned from Vietnam just six months before. "If you don't mind me saying so," my mother said, "your son needs help. I'd get him in to see somebody right away before he winds up in serious trouble. I mean serious. Next time Roy just might get himself shot." At the time I thought she had done the gracious thing, as she could've just as easily called my dad and had him arrested. But later that morning he caught it in a big way from his mother. It's hard to say what would've been worse. They lived in the apartments next door to our house, and come dawn, when he found the courage to come home, I heard them hollering. I looked out my window and saw Roy and his mother down in the carport. In his arms he carried a cardboard box with two puppies in it. Mrs. Lambert was right at his heels, screaming at his ear. She had on her bathrobe and slippers and between her fingers she held a lighted cigarette. Roy had long, thin hair and he didn't like to shave. He wore his old Army field jacket.

"You're sick," she said. "You're a real goddamn sicko, Roy."

"Shut up," he said.

She slapped him in the back of his head and it mussed up his hair. "Don't tell me to shut up," she said. "Don't you ever tell me to shut up." Again she slapped him on the back of the head, this time when he leaned over to unlock the door to his car. It was an old beat-up Riviera with the hood all primer gray.

"Don't touch me," he said. "I'm warning you, Mom. Do not fucking touch me."

"What'll you do?" she said. "Big tough soldier boy want to hit his mother? You disgust me, Roy. Tell me. What in God's name is the matter with you?"

Roy just shook his head, as if he didn't know either. Then he put the box with the puppies up front, climbed behind the wheel and shut the door. The back seat was already full of stuff, clothes mostly, stacked and shoved against the glass, and by the looks of it he had the trunk packed too. The frame squatted on its axles and I was sure the rear end would scrape the ground when he pulled out of the driveway. Mrs. Lambert flicked her cigarette at the car and it bounced off the hood in a shower of sparks. She shook her fist at him.

"Go on," she screamed. "Get those stinking dogs out of here. I don't want to see your face again."

All that day and the next, I found myself feeling sorry for Roy. Certainly I knew he had done wrong. Certainly I believed he deserved to be punished. In no way whatsoever did I side with Roy Lambert. But I was only eleven years old at the time and I admired him as a soldier, as I had admired my brother, who did not make it home that year or any other.

They were friends, not necessarily the best of friends. They hung out together now and then, and when Roy found himself in trouble with his mother he generally turned to Gerard for advice or help. Once when Roy was fourteen she found a lid of marijuana hidden in his steel-toed boot under the bed and hit him with the heel. He came over to our house worked up and crying, this big kid already practically twice his mother's size, his lip split and bleeding, and asked Gerard, begged really, if he could stay with us for the night until he figured out what to do. Gerard asked our mother and she said it was okay by her. But at this point in time our parents were still together and our father's word was the rule. He was a beat cop for the LAPD and when he came home from work and learned what had happened he told Gerard he didn't think it was such a great idea, sleeping here instead of straightening things out with his mother.

"It's better," he said, "just to settle up now. You know she wants you home."

Gerard took our father aside in the hallway.

"But she beat the hell out of him," he said.

"How she disciplines her boy is none of your damn business or mine."

"Look at his face."

"Look nothing," he said. "The kid is on drugs. I don't want him in this house. Remember something now. I could arrest him if I want."

He let Roy stay for dinner, but when we were eating dessert he phoned Mrs. Lambert and told her to come get him. If he mentioned the beating, I didn't hear it. As for Roy's old man, he never talked about him and my brother and I knew better than to ask. All this is to say I felt a certain responsibility for Roy Lambert, small as it may have been, and when I came across him asleep in his car I decided to do what I could.

This happened a few days after he was kicked out.

I found him parked under the bridge at Fourth Street next to the Los Angeles River. Railroad tracks ran nearby. Inside the car one of the pups rested on his chest with its eyes half closed. The other gnawed at the upholstery in the back seat. They were some kind of mix—a cross between a doberman, say, and a mongrel shepherd. They were maybe ten, eleven weeks old. I tapped on the window. Roy opened his eyes quickly, though he didn't look startled, as I would've expected, waking him under these circumstances. I pointed to the back seat.

"That one there," I said. "He's ripping your car all to pieces, Roy."

The pup on his chest looked at me and growled. Roy sat up and drew both his hands over its head, slowly and firmly, so it made the skin taut and the eyes narrow. Then he cooed in its ear.

"Get 'im," he said. "Get 'im."

It growled deep from the throat and bared its teeth. Roy rolled down the window and grinned. The pup looked more cute than fierce, but in a few weeks that would change.

"Protection," Roy said. "Protection, man." He petted it gently on the chest. "She's going to be one mean bitch someday."

"My mom and I could use one like her," I said. "A good watchdog like that."

Roy looked away, and for a moment there I wished I hadn't said anything.

"You want, you can have her. She's half wolf, you know. Worth money," he said. "This one here is a real fighter."

I may have been young but I was smart enough to

know that pup didn't have any more wolf in it than my mother's old Pekingese. I looked down at my feet and then back up at Roy. "You need a place to stay," I said, "I can help you out. It'd be better than sleeping in this car." He cocked his head and gave me a curious look. His left eye lid drooped, naturally, and reminded me faintly of the retarded.

Roy continued to pet the puppy in his lap.

"Where is it?" he said. "This place."

I nodded at the river.

"Man," he said, "don't be messing with me."

"I ain't messing with you, Roy," I said.

The pup jumped off his lap.

"C'mere," he said to it. "C'mere, baby."

Roy locked up the car and followed me. Over the fence. Across the railroad tracks. We saw the different entrances clearly now, spaced about every hundred yards up and down the concrete embankment of the river, these black holes cut deep into the earth and closed over, at certain times of the year, with heavy iron grates that looked like cat heads from a distance. The one near Fourth Street had rusted off its hinges and I led Roy past it, into the dark open mouth of the tunnel. It ran, like the others, far beneath the city, there were all kinds of turns and once you made it past the first one it was dark, so dark you couldn't see your hand if you held it right up to your face. I had a flashlight stashed at the entrance. Sometimes I used it, sometimes I didn't.

Above us, as Roy and I made our way through the darkness, we could hear the soft rush of the cars on the freeway overhead.

"This is a sewer," Roy said.

"It's no sewer," I said. "If it was it'd stink."

"It stinks," he said.

"Not bad," I said.

I aimed the flashlight down at our feet, more to Roy's than my own. The water was only at a trickle, though there were still plenty of spots that were always mossy, no matter the time of year, where you could slip and crack your skull if you weren't careful. Everything was concrete. The walls, the floor, even the channel outside where the water drained into that thing called the L.A. River. In the winter, when the rains fell hard, the tunnels filled with the dirty water from off the streets above and rushed and slapped against the walls. The noise, it was incredible. But it was summer now, June, there was no water to fill our boots and push against our legs as we walked, and except for the darkness, Roy and I had no trouble.

We turned a corner and I shined the light down another tunnel. It faded before it fell on anything. "Shit," Roy said. "I hope you know where the hell you're going." I told him not to worry. He stopped to light a cigarette. When he struck a match the flame lit up his face in a way that made his eyes look empty and the lines in his cheeks sharp, as if the skin had been stretched too tightly over the bone. "There used to be this place in Hollywood," he said. "On the Boulevard, this hotel. It was all boarded up and the whores and the junkies used to crash there. They called it Hotel Hell. I stayed there one time when my mom found my lid. You taking me back to Hotel Hell?" I laughed. I told him no and we walked on. Cholos had written all over the walls when you started into the tunnels, and there was even some the first quarter mile or so back. But we were beyond that now and it was just too dark for most, not even the local homeboys, to bother going further. I once found a woman's panties about twenty yards from the mouth of one tunnel that let out near Griffith Park. Another time I found three brass casings from a .38 and a yellow shirt stiff with blood on the sleeve. We made another turn.

The vault was roughly a half-mile into the tunnels, counting turns, and though I don't know for sure I think it had been abandoned years before because of a fire. The walls still smelled like smoke, and most of the wiring, what the electricians couldn't cut and pull and sell for the copper, had melded to the panels. If I shined my flashlight close on the connections you could see what looked like powder burns from a gun fired point blank, where the wires had sparked and caught fire. The walls, like the tunnel walls, were concrete and the door was made of iron. I opened that door now and let Roy walk in first. I had a Coleman lantern and I lit it for us. I had a cot, I had an old overstuffed chair and some blankets, I had a wood TV cabinet for a coffee table, a radio and a stash of corned beef hash, tomato soup and canned spaghetti. I had a few bottles of Coca-Cola, two gallons of fresh water in plastic jugs, a switchblade that once belonged to my brother, and a stack of *Playboys* I'd found at the city dump.

I opened a bottle of Coke and took a drink and passed it to Roy. Then I sat down in the chair, crossed my arms behind my head and smiled. Roy squatted on his haunches.

"How'd you ever find this place?" he said.

"Exploring," I said. "Just wandering."

Roy wagged his head. "Tunnel man," he said, "tunnel rat." He smiled. "You are the Tunnel Man. You are the Rat Boy," he said. "Your bro, he would've been proud, man."

"I don't like to talk about him," I said.

"You got to talk," Roy said.

"Talking don't do shit," I said.

"Hey, man," he said. "Who told you that?"

I shrugged.

"The gooks," he said, "they got these tunnels and somebody got to climb down there and flush 'em out. That's your bro. Boom," Roy said. "Boom fucking boom boom boom, man. Head first with a double barrel shotgun and a flashlight. You got to be crazy. Got to be one brave bad mother. Your brother," he said, "your brother, man. He was all right. He was a good tunnel rat."

"That how he die?" I said.

"How do you think?"

"Nobody ever said. My mom doesn't like to talk about it. Same with my old man."

Roy looked at me and frowned.

"You keep climbing down those tunnels you ain't going to keep coming back up." He took a long swallow from the Coke and handed it back to me. "I don't care how good you are, somebody got your number, man. Somebody always got your number, and they just waiting for you to come knocking."

"Did they get him?" I said. "The son of a bitch who killed my brother? Did they blow his ass away?"

"It don't make a difference," he said. "Put it out of your mind, man. Gerard was all right. Gerard was cool. He died good." Roy reached inside the collar of his shirt. He lowered his head and worked a necklace over his ears and handed it to me.

"Go on," he said. "Try it on."

The necklace was made of a couple of dozen or so blackened and gnarled teeth strung together on a piece of thin rawhide. They were small teeth. I thought they might've once belonged to a boy around my age, or maybe an old woman.

"Put your hand on the wall," I said.

"What for?"

But he did it.

"You feel it?" I said. "Shut your eyes."

There were vibrations every now and then, when something heavier passed above us, an eighteen-wheeler or maybe a bus, and if I closed my eyes I saw the tires, as if through a sheet of glass, down to the very markings in the treads as they rolled over me, all thunder and exhaust, again and again. "Your brother," he said, "he was a good soldier. He was all right, man. He went down a hero." I opened my eyes. Roy still had his shut. The Coleman lantern made an ugly hissing noise. "I feel it now. Christ," he said. "Christ, they're crawling all over us. They're fucking everywhere."

The teeth clicked against each other, like beads, as I slipped them over my head.

For months after my brother's death everything in his room was left untouched. The shoes in his closet were neatly arranged on the floor just as he had left them, his bed was still perfectly made for his homecoming, and over his dresser rested a fine layer of dust. Sometimes I went into the room and sat there, on the edge of the mattress, and tried to picture him beside me—reading, or at his desk gluing together the small pieces of a model Camaro, maybe another jet fighter. He had a mobile of planes in a mock dogfight suspended over his bed. Sometimes I went to his closet, lifted one of his shirts to my face and smelled it for his scent. Other times, when my parents argued, I took Gerard's pillow and pressed it tight against my ears. I don't know whether or not my father had been planning to leave, if he had done it suddenly, or if Gerard's death simply put too much strain on the both of them. But this was the year he began drinking more than usual and staying out late, as often as not the entire night. This was the year he got drunk and dragged everything out of Gerard's room—the mattresses, the pictures on the wall, all his clothes—and loaded everything into the bed of his truck. My mother didn't try to stop him. There was no screaming. No big dramatics. There was hardly even a look of disapproval on her face. At the time I thought she was weak, that she was afraid of him. But I'm older now. I'm older and I wonder if in trying to destroy what memories were left of Gerard he hoped to salvage what he'd lost of himself. I wonder if my mother hadn't already known this, and that in not stopping him she'd hoped to save this sad thing they called their marriage.

She kept a picture, and when my father walked out the door one night for a drink and didn't return for two weeks, and then only to pick up his clothes, she brought it out and set it on its own table in the hallway. Gerard was dressed in his Marine's uniform, just a headshot with the close-cropped hair, and he'd done without the smile. Tonight, as she did every night, after she checked the locks on the doors and turned out the lights, and after she had tucked me into bed, she stopped in the hallway to look at him. She'd been drinking and she let her finger trace the brim of his hat, down the side of his face, then slowly along the shoulder. My door was open a bit, and as I lay in bed with the necklace of teeth in my fist, I watched her purse her lips and gently blow the candles out one at a time. I listened to the sound her slippers now and again made catching at the toe and brushing the carpet as she turned her back to me and disappeared into her bedroom. I pulled the blanket up around my neck, held the teeth tight in my fist and tried to think of nothing. There was a freeway that ran near our house and I listened to the rush of the cars. Over and over I told myself the noise was only imaginary and that if I wanted to sleep all I had to do, all I had ever had to do, was will it into silence. I slipped the necklace under my pillow. It didn't matter that the teeth may have belonged to someone other than my brother's killer. What mattered, I thought, was that if he had to die, as he did, that he'd fought and fought hard and that he had passed bravely from this world to the next.

In the morning my father came by the house with a shotgun. It could've been Mrs. Lambert reported Roy to the police and that was how he found out. Could've been my mother mentioned the incident to a friend of theirs and it got back to my father through the grapevine. But he was there in uniform and he had his partner, a young man with a new haircut that made his ears look too big, wait outside for him in the patrol car. My mother answered the door in her bathrobe. She'd just washed her hair and had it wrapped it in a towel on her head. He had the gun in his hand.

"Get it out of here," she said.

My father nodded to the apartments next door.

"The next time," he said, "you might need to shoot the punk."

"That's a fine way for a cop to talk."

"I'm only looking out for you."

"Since when?" she said. "We haven't heard from you in six months, Jack. I personally couldn't give a damn.

But maybe your son might like to hear from you occasionally. It only takes a minute to call, or is that asking too much?"

He opened the screen door and let himself in. My mother tightened the sash on her robe. He set the shotgun down on the breakfast bar and held open his arms to me. "Hey," he said, "you got a hug for your dad?" He was a big man with strong wide shoulders and a pink face, a face pink not so much because he was an Irishman, but because of his drinking. I went to him and gave him a hug and he lifted me off the ground. "Long time no see. Who's this boy here," he said, and smiled. "Handsome and strong. Can't beat that." He held me tight against his chest, and as he did I stared over his shoulder at the TV. On screen Lucille Ball was working in a candy factory, at a conveyor belt, and soon it began to speed up so the candies, all these chocolates, came faster and faster. "Hey," my father said. He shook me a little. "Hey, why so stiff?" Lucy shoved chocolates into her mouth as they came off the conveyor belt, because she didn't know what else to do with them. The canned laughter grew louder. My father sighed and put me back down. His voice was serious.

"When did Lambert get back?" he said.

"I don't know," my mother said. "A year ago?"

"You know what gets me?"

"A lot of things get you, Jack."

"You know what I mean," he said.

But she was looking at the TV.

"That a pervert made it home and our boy didn't."

"C'mon," she said.

"He'll never amount to diddly and you damn well know it." My father picked up the gun and turned it with his hands. "Most of the time you scare people like him off, they won't come back. They're cowards," he said, "nothing but cowards. But then again you never can tell. Roy's not all there." He reached into his pocket and took out a handful of shotgun shells and placed them on the breakfast counter. "I got a right to know you can take care of our boy. Grant me that, Sally. You got to grant me that."

I didn't know much about guns then, and I don't know a great deal now, but I know at least this: it was a short barrel twelve-gauge Winchester, the kind the cops carry in their cars, what they call a riot gun that fires a wide spread from a short stance so that really all you have to do is more or less point it in the direction of the person you want to shoot and you're likely to hit him. Whether my mother only wanted to pacify my father to get him out of the house, or if after Roy came around she really felt a need for the gun, I can't say. But instead of arguing she let him show her how to slip the shells into the chamber and then how to clear it, scattering them across the floor when he worked the pump. I collected the shells off the carpet, the quarter brass casings cool in my hand, each heavy with lead shot. What I thought they offered us, these shells to my mother and me, this gun, was an odd sense of power and danger. My father stood behind her. "Keep it tight to your shoulder," he said. He put his hand under hers, the one she held under the pump, and as she pressed her cheek to the stock and sighted down the barrel he lingered over her for a moment, enough only to take in the white curve of her neck and the hair that rested there, along the smooth line of collar bone. He inhaled slowly, he inhaled evenly and deeply.

"Now," he said, "go ahead. Squeeze the trigger."

The canned laughter roared. Lucy pulled at her hair.

When my father left that morning I went to see Roy. I didn't use the flashlight to find my way. I had learned it by counting the turns and by feeling the welds in the pipe joints and memorizing how some were thick and some were flat and counting off my footsteps from there. I knew by listening to the rush of cars above me and the vibrations they made in the walls and by the sounds of the falling water from some distant and invisible storm drain. From Fourth Street to Broadway, I could feel my way through the tunnels, and if I wanted pull myself up through the gutter and look through the heavy iron grill at all the people, hundreds of them, crossing back and forth, this magnificent cacophony of shoes striking asphalt, of engines idling and bits of passing conversations and the rustle of clothing and newspaper. Who would look down to see me, this boy's head in the gutter, only the eyes staring up at you.

There used to be these ads for X-ray vision glasses in the back of my comic books, and when I was even younger I dreamed that if I owned a pair I could see through people's clothes, and in their nakedness view the soul and know what they thought and how they truly felt. But I knew better even then and by eleven I was certain that I would come closer to reconciling my differences with the world above me by remaining in my place beneath it. In this respect, Roy Lambert and I could well have been one and the same. I found him in the vault that morning, sitting on the cot and cradling one of the puppies in his arms, holding its head close against his chest. It didn't look well. The mean one, the bitch, bared its teeth and barked at me.

"Hush," Roy said. "Hush now."

He swatted her. I nodded at the pup in his lap.

"What's a matter with that one?"

"I don't know," Roy said. "She was doing fine the other day. She got some kind of bug, maybe." He wagged his head. "I just don't know, man."

There was a milky white film over its eyes, and it was skinny, so skinny you could see all of its ribs and the knobs, the unevenness of its tiny skull. I adjusted the gas on the lantern. Roy had it up too high.

"My dad gave my mom a gun this morning," I said.

"So what's that supposed to mean?" he said.

"Nothing," I said. "I'm just talking."

He stroked the sick dog, he cooed in its ear. I kneeled and looked at the other one. "I thought he took off when Gerard died," Roy said. "I thought they split up then." I told him he was right but that it didn't mean my father didn't come by now and then. "Your old man," he said, "he never cared much for me and I can't say I feel a whole lot different about him."

I reached over to the mean pup and scratched her behind the ear. She'd warmed up to me and in play, her teeth, like needles, gently broke the skin on my hand. The sick pup moaned.

"Goddamn," Roy said, "I hate to see him get sick."

On the Fourth of July I got drunk for my first time and threw a Cascading Fountain as high into the sky as I could and watched it tumble to the earth in a trail of white spark, hissing as it fell past us and finally exploding in a burst of even greater light on the concrete below. We'd lit it, this fountain, on the bridge overlooking the Los Angeles River. We were reeling, we were laughing. Roy jumped on top of the railing and held his arms out to his sides and flapped them up and down. He had on his army jacket with no shirt under it and the baggy sleeves fluttered in the wind.

"Get down from there," I said.

"I bet I could make it," he said.

"Make what?" I said.

"The water," he said.

The river was a narrow channel, maybe ten feet wide, and no more than a few feet deep. It was about a seventy foot drop.

"Roy," I said, "get down."

He smiled at me.

"You think your brother could do it?"

"My brother's dead," I said. It was the first time I had ever said it aloud, and I surprised myself. For awhile we were both quiet. Behind us the cars rushed by. One honked at Roy. "You're fixing to join him," I said, "if you don't get your ass down from there." I finished my beer and opened another. We had three cans left and half a box of Red Devil fireworks.

"What if he was still alive?" he said. "Ever think of that? What if they made a mistake?"

"I went to his funeral," I said.

"You see the body?"

"No," I said.

"Well," he said, "how can you be so sure if you didn't really see? Sounds to me like you're taking the word of the U.S. government and nobody in their right mind does that." He shook his head. "All I'm saying is what if, what if they sent back the wrong body and he's still down there? Still wandering around the tunnels." He rocked on his heels.

"Maybe he's happy down there. Maybe he likes it. You think of that? He never hated the gooks, anyway, not enough, and you got to just do it, not think."

Roy began to walk along the rail again. He looked down at me and grinned. "You got to move like the river, you got to rush like the wind."

He held out his arms, as if he were reaching for something. His voice rose. "Hand me a volcano, man. Light me a Piccolo Pete. Give me a fucking Roman Candle." I passed him the Roman Candle and he lit it with his cigarette. The fuse hissed. Roy pointed it to the sky as the tip opened with a kick of blue flame. He leaned back and went into a wind up, making circles with the flame—once, twice, three time—before he sent it up. It rose higher and higher and then, hanging frozen in the air for a long moment, all whites and reds against the night sky, turned on itself and began finally to fall. Suddenly Roy saw something else, caught it out of the corner of his eye. He jumped to the sidewalk. I turned around. A black-and-white idled at the curb. I heard the flap of Roy's jacket, the spit of gravel under his shoes. But I just stood there like a fool, my heart pounding. There were street lamps spaced along the bridge about every hundred feet or so, and each time Roy passed under one I kept half expecting, half hoping for him to look back, maybe wave me on. Any kind of sign would've done. But he never stopped. Never even turned around. The last time I saw Roy Lambert he was crossing the bridge and then he disappeared back under it. Down to the river, back to the tunnels. Over the railing, on the concrete below, the Roman Candle lay busted on the concrete, the tube uncoiled but still sending out sparks of red and white.

As the cop slipped out from behind the wheel I saw that it was my father's partner, the man with the big ears. He shined his flashlight in my face. He sighed.

"I thought a cop's son would know better," he said.

"How much you been drinking?"

"I just had one beer."

"Who you kidding?" he said.

"Nobody," I said.

The police radio crackled.

"That's right," he said. "Your friend, the rabbit. Why'd he run?"

"I don't know."

"He got something to hide?"

"I don't know," I said.

A Buick passed on the street and the driver slowed down and leaned over the wheel to get a better look at me. "Wipe that smile off your face," the cop said, "and get in the car." If I was smiling, I didn't know it. The muscles around my mouth felt stiff, my lips numb. I started toward the patrol car.

"What's that around your neck?" he said. "What the hell are those things?"

My mother made me give up the necklace, it was "sick," she said, and what happened to it after that I have no idea. But I still sometimes feel it around my throat with the teeth resting on my chest, these gnarled little bits of bone. I still sometimes see myself in my old bed, staring up at the ceiling and listening again to the soft rush of cars as they passed on the freeway. I thought of my brother that night. I thought of Roy Lambert. I closed my eyes and fell asleep and when I woke my head was burning with fever. All that morning and the next I moved in and out of consciousness, waking only long enough to take the thick, dry aspirins that my mother lifted to my lips and swallow them with a wince and a sip of cool water. On the third day, in the evening, my father came by. I heard his footsteps in the hallway, and when the door was opened I felt the light on my eyelids, a pulsing, a flutter of splintered colors. "Don't wake him up," my mother said. "He's still running a temperature. If it doesn't break by morning I'm taking him to the hospital." Then the room fell dark again. She led him to the kitchen and offered him a drink. He pulled up a chair. The legs scraped the linoleum.

"You don't have to worry about Roy Lambert," he said. "He won't be looking in anybody's windows, not for a while anyway."

"What'd you do?"

"Exactly what I said."

"Smart," she said. "Real smart. Now he has a good reason to get even."

"Let him try."

"Easy for you to say."

"I don't want him near our boy. We already lost one."

"You should thank me," he said. "That son of a bitch could be a rapist."

"How bad did you hurt him?"

"Bad enough."

I heard her open a cupboard, then close it. "One of these days," she said. "One of these days, Jack, you're going to get thrown off the force."

There was a long pause. I imagined he took a sip of his drink and that he used the time to carefully measure his next words. I heard the clink of ice against glass. He was twirling it around.

"Sally," he said, "I've been thinking. I've been thinking pretty damn hard lately. The boy needs a man around the house and I'd like to come home."

"This isn't your home anymore."

"Come on now," he said.

"Come on nothing," she said.

Again there was a long pause. Again there was the scraping of the chair legs on the linoleum, only this time he had to be getting up. "We'll take it slow then," he said. "How about a movie this Friday? We can go to Petrino's for dinner. What do you say?" I bet he moved around the table to reach for her and I would bet that she stepped away.

"Sally?" he said. "Honey? What do you say?"

But I didn't hear her say anything.

*

When my mother went to sleep later that night I got dressed, slipped out the door and headed for the tunnels. Roy's car was where he usually parked it—under the Fourth Street bridge. But the windshield was shattered and the body looked like someone had taken a baseball bat to it. Inside the seats had been slit open with a knife and the headliner ripped down. I felt my heart speed up. I felt my mouth go dry. At the entrance to the tunnel I found the flashlight and made my way back to the vault, running when I could, slipping sometimes on the moss, once falling.

"Roy," I shouted, as I got closer. "Roy, it's me." But even then I think I already knew. The door to the vault was open and I shined my flashlight inside. The cot had been overturned. The TV cabinet had been smashed, the overstuffed chair slit open so that the guts of it hung free, and the *Playboys* were ripped up and scattered across the floor. I looked at the wreckage and I thought of my father, I thought of his fury and I saw his Irish face, all vicious and twisted with anger, the tight pale lips turned up in a grimace, his shirt sleeves neatly rolled to the elbow so he could swing his arms better, the police baton better. On his breath was the sour stink of whiskey, and his eyes, narrowed, hardly looked like eyes at all lost in the bloated and swollen flesh of his cheeks. The air smelled rotten. I heard a low rumbling noise that began in the dog's stomach and worked its way up to the throat as a snarl. Its voice had grown deeper and I couldn't tell right away, not for sure, if it was behind or ahead of me. It growled again, low and even, deep from its throat. "Calm down, boy," I said. "Calm down." But any second, I thought, any second it was going to bite, put its teeth into my leg, my arm. The growling grew louder, closer. I shined the flashlight around the room, ahead of me, behind me, and that's when I saw it. The other dog, the sick one. It lay on its side on the floor. The flesh had been gnawed from its bones but a few strips, dry and twisted, still held fast to the white bits of skull. Now the other dog came out from behind it, around from the footing of the cot, and snapped at me. I held the flashlight in its eyes and they glowed a yellowish-white phosphorescent. Its teeth were bared. It snapped at me again and I stepped back. "You want it," I said, "you can have it. Nothing left anyway." The dog lunged. Its teeth grazed my pants leg and I felt its warm moist breath on my ankle and I thought of kicking it, hurting it, killing it even. Instead I backed away, slowly, until I was out of the vault. The dog stopped in the doorway. I didn't get much further. It was as if my stomach had a will of its own and wanted to come up out of my throat.

In the morning my mother came in to see how I was getting along. She sat on the edge of my bed and placed her hand on my forehead. Her skin felt cool and soft against mine. I'd slept fitfully, if I slept at all, but by dawn I knew my fever had finally broken. I told her I was feeling better, a whole lot better, and she let her hand slip from my forehead, down along my cheek. I told her I had a dream and that it was about Roy and that something bad had happened to him. She'd been smiling but at the mention of his name the smile disappeared.

"I don't want you talking about him," she said. "I don't want you even mentioning his name. Understand?"

"I understand," I said.

"Good," she said.

"But he's okay?"

"Far as I know."

If I couldn't get the truth from my mother, I would get it somewhere else. I would find Roy myself and ask him. But his car remained under the bridge. I never saw him in the tunnels and I looked. I thought if he wasn't sleeping in his car or in the vault that maybe he had gone back to his mother. But that wasn't so.

It was two weeks before I finally worked up the courage to ask Mrs. Lambert what had become of Roy. I paid her a visit in the afternoon. The day was hot and her screen door was open and I could smell chicken frying in the kitchen.

In the living room Mrs. Lambert sat on a brand new La-Z-boy chair in front of the TV. It was a big chair and she was a small, skinny woman all bones and sharp angles, so that for a moment, from the side at least, she reminded me of a child. A game show was on and the sound was turned up high. I must have stood there a minute, looking in on her, trying to work myself up to say something. Between her fingers burned a cigarette, the ash growing longer, so long I thought it would break and fall. But she raised it to her lips in time, took a long last drag, then put it out in the ashtray balanced on the armrest of the chair. I thought she might have been a pretty woman at one point in her life, long ago, but now she looked old, a mean kind of old that came from too much bitterness. Finally she turned and took note of me.

"Look," I said, "I'm just wondering about Roy."

"What about him?"

"You know. Where he's at?"

"Why don't you ask your father?" she said.

My father had been in the wrong. I didn't know what to say.

"I'm sorry about him," I said.

"Sorry don't pay the hospital bill."

She lit another cigarette and stared at the TV again.

"What hospital is he at?" I said.

She turned in her chair and looked at me with those little eyes of hers. She had shaved the brows and penciled them in. I saw the bones in her forehead.

"He's gone again," she said. "God bless his soul he makes it home. Two times around is pushing your luck, wouldn't you say?" I nodded. I thought now that I should leave, and I would have if she had paused a second longer. "I don't know what your parents told you and I don't care. But your brother never would've been half the soldier my boy Roy is, even if he ever made it to the front. I know what he was made of and it wasn't the same stuff."

"What're you talking about?" I said.

"He just didn't have it."

"What're you talking about?" I said, louder.

"Don't you raise your voice to me," she said. "You

can just get the hell out of here."

"My brother died fighting," I said. "He killed all kinds of people before they could take him down."

Mrs. Lambert looked at me again. She looked at me hard. I know now in those few seconds before she spoke that if she were any of kind of woman she would've had to think against it, and maybe if my father had never beaten the hell out of Roy Lambert and put him in the hospital she would've kept silent.

"You can believe anything you damn well please," she said. "We all got to believe, I guess. Believe, sometimes, just to believe." Then she turned and looked at the TV. "Now you go remind your father," she said. "You go remind him if he forgot."

I left then and went back to the tunnels. I didn't want to talk with my father. I didn't want to talk with my mother. I wanted to give the one dog a proper burial and the other a meal. I had been feeding it over the weeks, leaving it dry food and table scraps when I could. But every time I tried to get the corpse the other dog stood over it, snarled and snapped at me. Once I thought I had made friends with it again, to where I could almost pet it. But when I stepped just a little too close it growled and bit at me. Then one day, this day now years past, I came back and found it was gone. I don't know if it lived or died, or if like the pet Cayman that gets sucked into the sewer it found its way into the darkness to grow and thrive on the rats and the human waste. But it is possible. It could be down there now, and in a way a part of me still is. The war ended before I was old enough to enlist, yet I believe I would've made a fine soldier, as my brother and Roy had, and though I know it's senseless and selfish to wish the blood had poured a little longer so that I could've been a part of it, I nonetheless feel I was somehow denied.

Roy didn't return, but neither was his body ever found. I believe that he made his home there. I believe that he's alive and well. Every now and then I imagine the great rush of water from the winter storms, pouring down off the streets and into the gutters, and the tremendous noise it makes slapping against the tunnel walls. Every now and then I hear the sound of it, like the keen of an animal that has never seen the sky, coming from somewhere out of the darkness.

I hear it over and over again until I can't catch my breath.

THE FRIEND

a short story

1

I hadn't used for about two years when I got a call from Lorraine. It was close to one in the morning and my wife and I had been sound asleep. "You got to come over," Lorraine said. "Right now. Dana's locked himself in the van with Sandy and he won't come out." She sounded pretty shook up. "You're his only friend," she said. "You got to come over right now. I don't know who else to ask."

My wife, she didn't like the idea.

"Jesus Christ, he did what?"

"You heard me," I said.

"I really don't want you going over there."

She shook her head, as if judging.

"I don't think there's anything to worry about," I said. "Dana wouldn't hurt her."

"I wouldn't put it past him," she said. "You just better let Lorraine call the cops, let them take care of it."

Our child, in the room next to ours, shifted in his sleep and bumped against the wall. Julie gave me a look. "Please," she said. "Please, don't do this to me again." She patted the mattress. "Come on, come on back to bed, honey," she said. "I really don't want you going over there."

But I thought I should at least drive by their place. Dana and I had both been close to the edge more than once together and I owed him. The lamp on the nightstand was on, and before I turned it off I reached under the blanket and put my hand on her belly. I tried to give her a kiss goodbye, but she rolled over on her side. "Don't be that way," I said. "I'll be home as soon as I can." She ignored me though, she was mad, so there was nothing for me to do but leave. On my way down the hall I stopped to check on our kid and found him uncovered, the blankets kicked down around his feet. The window was open and the big flood light above the next-door neighbor's garage shined across his face. He was only nineteen months but sometimes, at moments like these, when his hair stuck up in the back, fuzzy from sleeping on it, he reminded me of a miniature old man, a feeble one. I closed the window, made sure it was locked, and then covered him back up.

Outside, in the driveway, I heard the faint sound of laughter from a television. It was coming from Mr. Breslin's house, the old widower across the street. The night was warm, he had his front door open and the blue and grey light of the TV flickered against the living room drapes. I figured the screen door was locked. But I still thought, as I got into my car and drove away, that even if the neighborhood was safe it still wasn't a good idea. It still wasn't what you'd call smart. Anyone at any time, anyone with a sharp pointed knife could slice through the screen, quickly and easily, with hardly a noise.

2

They lived in the San Fernando Valley, off Ventura Boulevard in North Hollywood. There was a liquor store on the corner run by an old Korean and his son, and sometimes, before it closed at two in the morning, Dana and I used to walk down there and pick up beer and whiskey to take the edge off the high. He liked to gripe about the kids that were still hanging around in front of the laundromat just up the block.

"You think those little pricks are washing clothes? Look at that one. Ten, maybe, at the most. The little shit ought to be home. If it was my kid I'd kick his ass good."

They wanted to move but they had lived there for as long as Julie and I had known them, and at the rate things were going I didn't see how they could've managed any differently. Dana was an electrician at Lorimar before he was fired for stealing cans of film off the trailers. Instead of reporting him to the cops, the executive producer on the show put the word out on him around the studios. I don't know what was worse, criminal charges or unemployment, but one thing was clear: he hadn't worked in a long time. The film was worth hundreds of dollars a roll and before they caught him he was selling it to a rock video producer in the Valley. Dana made enough on the side to buy himself a Harley, and he and Lorraine had some real good times taking it out down PCH, or up to the San Bernardino mountains where they had some friends, where

I think he bought their stuff, speed mostly from the bathtub chemists.

My wife, she didn't like motorcycles, she didn't like the way Dana and Lorraine lived, or how they raised their daughter, and she'd quit using drugs when she found out she was pregnant. That was three years ago, and to her credit she hadn't touched anything since, except for a glass of wine now and then. Julie and I were originally from Sacramento, we lived in a little trailer park just west of Highway 5, and for a while there after we packed up and moved south we didn't know anybody. We didn't have any friends. Those were some pretty lean times, too, financially. But I finally landed a decent job with the telephone company and we moved again, out of the apartments behind Lorraine and Dana. With the new baby and my job and all there just wasn't much time for anything else, including ourselves. I hadn't seen Dana in over a year, and then it was by coincidence at the Lucky's Market. He was picking up a head of cabbage and a corned beef.

"Lorraine's favorite," he said. "It's her birthday and I want to surprise her."

I thought about inviting them over later for a couple of drinks. But the last time they visited Lorraine and my wife had a big run-in, and she made it clear they weren't welcome around anymore. Julie had thought, or maybe she'd only hoped, that when we moved out of the neighborhood we wouldn't see them again, that we had left them behind like the other things you throw out when you're packing, the stuff you don't see any use in hauling around anymore, like old furniture when you can finally afford new.

3

The front porch light was on. Lorraine sat on the steps waiting for me and smoking a cigarette. It was September, an Indian summer, and she had on shorts and a halter top. Her feet were bare. The van was parked in the driveway and from a distance it looked like some kind of dragster, the way it leaned forward. But when I walked closer I saw that the two front tires were flat. She noticed me looking at them.

"The son of a bitch," Lorraine said, "he's not going anywhere. I let the air out." Then she shouted at the van. "Frank's here, Dana. I hope you're happy." To me, she said, lowering her voice, "I didn't want to call you but he's really freaked out. He keeps saying there's Filipinos up on the roof."

"What?"

"Filipino guys," she said. "Half a dozen of them. I told you he's really freaked out. Talk to him," she said. "I've had it."

I went to the van and tapped on the window on the driver's side. It was dark inside and there was a curtain drawn behind the seats of the cab so you couldn't see in back.

"Dana," I said. "You want to tell me what's going on?"

He didn't answer.

"Listen," I said. "I didn't drive all the way out here to talk to myself. I mean it's pretty goddamn extreme locking yourself up with your kid."

There was movement in the van, so that it rocked a bit, and a second later his face appeared in the window on the driver's side. His eyes were wide, wild looking, and he was sweating.

"Open the door," I said.

"Go to hell," he said. "Mind your own business."

"Come on," I said. "Open it. I don't want to talk through a window all night."

"Then leave."

"Is Sandy okay?" I said.

"She's fine. We're both fine," he said.

"Maybe you ought to let her speak for herself," I said.

"She's sleeping," he said.

His face disappeared from the window. I stepped back from the van so I could talk to Lorraine in private. I lowered my voice.

"How long's he been in there?"

"Since this afternoon," she said. "I think he finally went off the deep end."

"Did he do that?" I said.

Her left eye was swollen with a purple half-moon under it.

"Who do you think?"

I shook my head in disgust.

"I don't know," she said. "I honestly just don't know anymore. Every day it's something. I mean look at the goddamn lawn even. Really, Frank, would you let your lawn go like that? All he does is sit on his ass all day watching TV. He doesn't even think of looking for work anymore. Now he pulls this crap." She raised her voice. "I'm fed up. You hear me, Dana? You hear that?"

I walked around to the back of the van and tried to look through the window, but it was tinted and I couldn't see anything. "Dana? Come on, man. Whoever was up on the roof," I said, "they're gone now."

"Bullshit."

"No bullshit," I said.

"They're up there," he said. "Mean little shits. One's got a knife, tailed me and Sandy home from the park. I'm not jerking you around. They're up there."

"Let your daughter out," I said. "You can stay there all night, I don't care. But let your daughter out. It isn't right, Dana. Besides," I said, "she's got school tomorrow."

A long silence passed.

"It's not safe," he said.

"See what I mean," Lorraine said. "He's lost it."

I gave her a look like we had to understand, like we had to be patient with him.

"It's not like before," Dana said. "When we used to walk down to the Korean's. It was bad then but it's worse now. Those kids, man. They got Uzi's now," he said, "they got AK's."

"Gone," Lorraine said. "Out to lunch."

"They'll blow your ass away for a fucking dime bag," he said.

"Fine language for your little girl," Lorraine said. "You set a real good example."

"You're one to talk," he said.

"Sandy," she said. "Can you hear me? Just hold tight, honey. We'll get you out of there."

"Like hell," Dana said.

Lorraine shouted, "I could have your ass right now for assault and battery if I wanted. One phone call."

"Both of you," I said. "Knock it off."

The phone rang inside the house and Lorraine ran to answer it. She left the door open and inside I saw magazines strewn all over the floor like someone had thrown them around in a fight. On the wall hung a Confederate flag and on the TV was an old lava lamp. Gobs of red wax, or whatever it was inside, floated slowly to the top then just as slowly slipped to the bottom. I walked back to the front of the van and tapped on the windshield. Dana's face appeared in the window again, and this time I noticed that he didn't have any shirt on. It had been a hot day, and in the van it must have been incredible.

"How much you been using," I said.

"You think I'm high?"

"Yeah, man," I said. "I think you're high. I think you're blowing it, too, and if you don't watch it you'll end up downtown."

He reached over and opened the glove compartment. A light came on. Inside was a sandwich bag about half full of coke, or it might have been meth. He held it up to the window for me to appreciate, but you couldn't tell much just by looking. I felt my pulse quicken. "Bolivian flake, our friend," he said. "Shaved off the kilo." Dana rolled the plastic between his fingers with the mouth of the bag open, so that the rocks inside caught the light. Up close, under a better light, the colors would've shined like the inside of an abalone shell. My hands began to sweat. Dana smiled. "Remember that two-day run," he said. "Sun up to sun down in my kitchen. You wouldn't take off your sunglasses." He laughed gently. "Last big blow out, buddy, all you could do, all you could want. Free. Before you moved to the other side of town and forgot who your real friends were. You remember." He nodded to himself. "I do, man. I remember my friends and I don't quit talking to them just because I think I'm better."

"Want me to go check the roof? If they're gone," I said, "will you come out?"

Sandy woke up then. I couldn't see her, but I heard her voice, frail and thick with sleep. She was six years old, his daughter from another marriage—to a woman that had left him for a marine, a vet with a bum leg, that when he walked made one look shorter than the other. I'd only met him once, while we were watching TV with the sound off, and he came over to make a buy.

"Daddy," she said, "when are we going to go?"

"Soon, baby," he told her. "Soon it'll all be better, honey. Go back to sleep." He waited until she was quiet again before he said anything else. The muscles in his jaws looked tense. His whole face looked tense. "I know why you're here." His voice cracked, in a strange way, and his eyes grew even wider. "Dana knows, man. Dana is no fool." I wanted to tell him that he was wrong about me, dead wrong and out of his mind, only I didn't feel so sure anymore.

Instead I said:

"Dana, I'm going to check the roof and if there's no one there, you're going to come out. We understand each other?"

Then Lorraine came back and she looked mad.

"That was Mrs. Lansen," she shouted. "She wants to know what's going on, Dana."

"What'd you tell her?" I said.

"To stick it."

"Great," Dana said. "Treat the neighbors like shit, too. You're a bitch, Lorraine. Frank," he said, "she's a genuine bitch, man."

I sighed, then took Lorraine by the arm and led her back a few steps from the van.

"Do you have a ladder?" I said.

She wrinkled her nose, she cocked her head, she looked at me like I was crazy. But I told her, "It's the blow, I know that," I said. "But I want to check just so I can say I did."

"Go ahead. I don't care, I don't give a damn. In fact," she said, "I'm not even sure why I bothered to call you anymore. Christ, you're just like him."

The way she turned on me, I didn't know what to say, so I headed around to the backyard. The ladder was already leaning against the side of the house. I climbed it and looked. The roof was a flat top with tar and gravel, like all the others on the block. The TV antenna framed the night sky. In the rain gutter was a tennis ball, and near the edge of the roof I found a plastic truck. I picked them up on my way down and tossed them on the patio. But when I got back to the front yard, I saw the van rock. I heard the axle give under his weight, I heard his daughter say something though I couldn't make out the words. The engine started. Lorraine pounded on the window. Dana slipped it into gear and the two front tires, flat, slapped, slapped against the pavement, and the van rolled down the driveway.

4

My wife and Lorraine had their big run-in the last time she and Dana visited. I'm still not sure exactly what set them off. They'd left Sandy with a babysitter, a fat girl named Marsha, a sixteen-year-old chainsmoker who used to live next door to us in the apartment complex in North Hollywood, and pulled up to our house late one Saturday afternoon, unannounced, on Dana's Harley. Julie and I were in the backyard. We were having a barbeque, and I'd just gotten the coals going when we heard the rumble and pop of the engine in our driveway.

"Oh shit," Julie said. "Tell them we have guests coming or something. I really don't feel up to seeing them, Frank."

She was seven months pregnant with Sean at the time, and moody, and I felt responsible to try and make things as easy as I could for her. But I was in a fix. Maybe they were being rude dropping in uninvited, but I was sure they didn't mean any harm by it. I didn't feel I could very well just send them away.

"Honey," I said. "One drink, okay?"

"They'll never leave."

She looked at me hard.

"I don't want them around here," she said. "As far as I'm concerned that part of your life is over and you better start picking your friends a little more carefully. You got a responsibility now to more than yourself." Then she added, in tone that summoned too much from the past, "I know what's going to happen. I know you, Frank."

I covered the steaks with some wax paper, so the flies wouldn't get to them, and then I went to the front yard through the side gate. The Harley ticked itself cool in the driveway. Dana wore a black leather vest over his Levi jacket. Lorraine had on a tank top without a bra under it, and in her arms she had a brown paper bag. I thought she was carrying a bottle of wine or a six pack, but it turned out to be something else.

Dana smiled at me, then looked at the house and spread his arms.

"Nice place," he said. "Why don't you pull a few strings and get me a job at the phone company." He winked at Lorraine. "Can you just see me in a suit and tie?" She punched him lightly in the arm and smiled. It wasn't a grand house, a little two bedroom place in Glendale, but it was ours, at least on paper. I kept the lawn mowed and the hedges trimmed and I'd just put on a fresh coat of paint the week before. It looked good and I appreciated Dana's gesture.

I led them around back to Julie, who was busy tossing the salad, and she greeted them warmly, enough anyway so you couldn't tell that she didn't want them here. Lorraine set the bag on the picnic table.

"We got you a house warming gift," she said. "A little late, but...."

She reached into the bag and took out a box wrapped in Christmas paper, with peppermint sticks and hollies on it.

"Come on," she said. "Open it. Every house needs one."

Julie wiped her hands on a paper towel and smiled. I headed to the kitchen to get them a beer. Dana followed me in.

"I got you a little house warming gift, too," he said, and immediately my heart speeded up. We did the stuff on top of the dresser in the master bedroom, and about thirty seconds later I completely lost my appetite. What I wanted now was to drink.

"Like old times, eh?" Dana said. He slapped me on the back. "How come you haven't been returning my calls, man?" I said I'd just been plain busy, that I'd been promoted to supervisor and he wasn't the only buddy I hadn't talked to in a hell of a long time. "Don't take it personally," I told him, and then I invited him to stay for the barbeque. At that point, high, I didn't see the harm in it. Julie, I thought she'd weather it. Dana and I did another line and then drove down to the grocery store to pick up beer and two more steaks. We did a line in my car in the parking lot, like a couple of stupid teenagers, looking this way and that for cops, then bending over the opened glove compartment, taking the speed into our noses, feeling it burn its way up.

I don't know what happened while we were gone, but when we came back, when we came through the gate laughing and having ourselves a time, Lorraine stood up from the picnic table. Her cheeks were flushed.

"Let's go, Dana."

"What're you talking about?" he said.

"We're not welcome here," she said. "I mean it. Let's go."

I looked at Julie, and though I didn't know who was at fault I had a strong feeling it was her. She just shook her head. She didn't say a word. "Whatever happened," I said, "let's just forget it." I tried to make light of it, whatever it was that set them off. "We got two fantastic steaks here, and if you haven't ever had a Frank Special you don't know what you're missing." I know it sounded corny but at the time I couldn't think of anything better. It was one of those moments when you know there's not a damn thing you can do to patch things up. But you still have to try, out of politeness if nothing else. "Let's all have a drink," I said. "One glass of wine isn't going to hurt the baby, Julie. My mother drank through her pregnancy and look at me," I said, making a stupid face, trying to get at least someone here to smile. I put my hand on her belly and thought I felt a kick inside. "I turned out fine," I said. Julie stepped back and narrowed her eyes at me.

"Shut up, Frank," she said.

"I'm just trying."

"I know what you're trying," she said. To Lorraine, she said, "And take your gift with you. I don't want it."

It was a lava lamp, and evidently before the fight started either my wife or Lorraine had thought enough of it to run an extension cord out from the garage and plug it in on the picnic table. Night was about to fall, and the light inside the lamp seemed unusually bright. The wax had begun to melt, and I watched a red glob of it stretch itself to the top. For a few seconds, or maybe it was longer, we all stood there watching it. Then Lorraine, before the glob broke and rose, stormed out of the backyard and slammed the gate behind her. Dana and I looked at each other. He rolled his eyes.

"Well," he said, "this is my cue."

Julie unplugged the lamp, wrapped the cord around it and handed it to him.

"Really, why don't you just keep it," she said.

"Honey," I told her.

"That's okay," Dana said. "That's okay. She's got a right."

I walked him out to the driveway.

"I'll call you later," I said. "I'm sorry, man. I don't know what's going on with her."

"She's got a right," he said again. Then he looked at the lamp in his arms. "Kind of dates us, doesn't it? This thing? But they're fun to watch when you're stoned." He got on the Harley. Lorraine had already straddled it. She wouldn't look my way. "We have to get going anyway," Dana said. "Marsha's babysitting and I don't trust her much." He paused. "Sandy, you know how she gets, man. Can't stand to be away from me." He laughed. "Everytime I split she thinks I'm never coming back."

"Daddy's little girl," Lorraine said, but it wasn't meant kindly.

When they left I went in the house and found Julie in the bedroom crying. I left her there, as I would again. I phoned Dana and invited myself over, thinking, wrongly, that all I wanted to do was apologize. But I was lying. I knew even then, as I was driving over to his place, that that wasn't the real reason.

For the next two days I sat in Dana's kitchen. Sun up to sun down. I didn't want to take off my sunglasses, and everything was tinted yellow. The linoleum floor, the walls, my hands, the Formica counter. Dana's face. Grocery bags full of empty beer cans and bottles were stacked next to the back door but we weren't fools, we knew better than to take them out. Through the window we spied a man parked in a car across the street, and every now and then, if we watched him closely, and we did, he turned in his seat and looked at us. He was pretending to read a newspaper.

I let the shades drop.

"It's a Plymouth," I said. "You know they always drive Plymouths. That's how you can tell. They have some kind of deal with Chrysler," I said. "It's a dead giveaway. Look for the little *e* on the license plate." We got Lorraine out of bed, it must've been six or seven in the morning, and made her peek out the window. She said it didn't have any *e*, but we knew that from this angle, from the window, that she couldn't really see the plate.

"You still better get rid of the stuff," I told Dana. "I mean it, man. The scale, the razors, everything." Better to be safe than sorry, we thought, and Dana wondered aloud why his own wife would be on their side. That set her off. She demanded to give me a ride home, before she dropped Sandy off at school, and when I refused because it was just too risky, she went to the phone and called Julie.

"I think you better come get your husband," she said. "He won't let me drive him. Dana's in no condition, either. Please," she said, "it's time he went home."

Dana left the room and a moment later—faintly, from down the hall—I heard the toilet flush. Sandy appeared in the doorway wearing a flannel nightgown with a picture of Donald Duck on the chest, and her curly hair sticking up in odd places. Then suddenly I heard the whack of helicopter blades circling above the house and I knew, beyond a doubt, with a certainty that made my heart freeze inside my chest for a beat, that it was all over. We had had it. There would be no ride home. This was the end.

"Listen," I said, as I dropped to one knee. "Can you hear them, honey? Listen. They're right on top of us now."

5

The van dipped down the driveway onto the street and tried to pick up speed. The flat tires continued to slap against the pavement, grinding against the rims with each revolution, so that soon the rubber began to smoke. You could smell it burning. Lorraine ran alongside the van and pounded on the back window with her fists and screamed. "You son of a bitch, you son of a bitch," she said. "I'm gonna kill you." Across the street a porch light flashed on and an old man in a bathrobe peered out from behind the drapes. Another light came on down the block. I ran to the window on the driver's side before he got too far. He couldn't go very fast with the two flat tires.

"Pull over," I shouted.

But he didn't listen, he stared straight ahead and kept on driving, as if I weren't there. I grabbed onto the side mirror and got my footing on the running board on the driver's side.

"Let go," he screamed. "I'm not messing around, man. This shit is for real. I swear it," he said. "I'll open the door and knock you on your ass." Though I believed him, I didn't let go. I hung on tighter. "I'll get on the freeway, I'll get on the fucking freeway and blow you off." Behind me Lorraine kept cursing and shouting, then I heard her slip, first her nails drag against the metal, then the whack of bone on asphalt when she hit. And then the sky lit up, all whiteness, so it hurt, so it blinded. From above a helicopter, from behind the spot of a black-and-white and ahead, cutting us off, another. He slammed on the brakes, it was either that or ram into one of the black-and-whites. But then he tried to back up and turn around, up onto someone's lawn, straight over the fence. It went down like tinder. I jumped before that and then they were out of their cars, these cops. Four or five of them, I think, to start. One took me from behind and knocked me to the ground.

I shouted, "That's my friend in the van."

"Shut up," the cop said, a young one—and strong—and he yanked my arms behind my back and cuffed my wrists so tight it cut into the skin. He smelled of cologne.

"Take it easy, man," I said, as if he would've listened at this point, as if he would've cared. "Don't hurt him. He's got his little girl with him but he's just high. I know him," I said. "He wouldn't do anything."

"Shut up," the cop said.

"The truth," I said. "We're friends."

"Just shut the fuck up."

The helicopter continued to circle above, the blades thrashing, whipping the sky, the beating deafening, with its bright white light aimed on the van. I heard one of the cops shout through a loudspeaker at Dana, warning, advising him to come out. The back door slowly opened. He held her in his arms and she clutched his neck and pressed her face tight against his chest. There was a tattoo on his forearm, a rattlesnake coiled to strike, a new one with the beads of dried blood still showing, and scattered across the floor of the van were Old Maid cards, the cartoon type for children, the big kind. Her feet dangled over her father's arm and turned inward slightly so that her toes touched. In her fist was a card, the grotesque caricature of the ancient queen of hearts. Dana's hair had come loose from its ponytail and covered all but one eye. He raised his chin.

"Here I am," he said.

But I don't think he was talking to the police. I don't think he was talking to any of us.

*

6

The motion sensor on the flood lamp above the neighbor's garage goes off as I coast up my driveway with the headlamps and the engine off. Light bathes the front yard, and if only for a moment it seems artificial in all its neatness and care. The lawn. The perfectly trimmed hedges. The white paint on the house still bright, not a chip, not a crack to be found. I get out of my car and go into the house and close the door quietly, ease the bolt into its sleeve, almost silently, hardly a noise. I'm proud of my skill but I wait a moment again, several, there in the living room, listening to my own breathing, listening to the hum of the refrigerator in the kitchen, listening to nothing to see if I've been successful. The digital clock on the VCR resting on the television says the time is 4:23 A.M. There's a pulsing behind my ears, pushing hard against the skin, and a slight ringing inside them. I pass my finger over the ridge of one ear to feel its heat. I imagine my face is flushed and I have trouble swallowing. I go to my son's room and find him again with the blanket kicked down around his legs, only this time I pick him up. I hold him against my chest and feel his heart pounding against mine. The rhythm is only slightly off. I smell his hair and the scent reminds me of my own and I take it in deep into my lungs. He turns his head to one side into my shoulder, he's not awake, his eyes remain closed, but the lids must feel the light from the neighbor's garage. He moans once, he kicks once and his knee brushes against my stomach. Then in the next room I hear my wife shift in her sleep, the sound of the mattress give beneath her, and I put our son back to bed and cover him up to his neck with only the sheet. The night, or the morning, it's still warm.

As I close the drapes on his window I spot an old Chevy Type II cruise by on the street outside. Its headlights are off, and I wonder what the driver is doing. I wonder if it's a man or a woman, if the headlights are only burned out, if the driver is drunk and has forgotten to turn them on, or if he's up to something. So I let myself outside again, quietly, and I go and stand on the lawn and I wait. I wait to see if he'll come back, and as I wait I notice a goddamn beer bottle on our lawn. The glass is shattered next to one of the sprinkler heads, the shards are brown and sharp and dangerous. It crosses my mind to pick up the pieces before someone else gets hurt. But I hesitate. I wait. I can't look away, not now, not again, not even for a moment.

THE TYPE IS PALATINO

BOOK DESIGN BY LYSA MCDOWELL
COVER PAINTING BY ALEXANDER RUDINSKY

PRINTING BY DATA REPRODUCTIONS